About Heidi Rice

Heidi Rice was born and bred and still lives in London, England. She has two boys who love to bicker, a wonderful husband who, luckily for everyone, has loads of patience, and a supportive and ever-growing British/French/Irish/American family. As much as Heidi adores 'the Big Smoke', she also loves America, and every two years or so she and her best friend leave hubby and kids behind and *Thelma and Louise* it across the States for a couple of weeks (although they always leave out the driving off a cliff bit). She's been a film buff since her early teens and a romance junkie for almost as long. She indulged her first love by being a film reviewer. Then a few years ago she decided to spice up her life by writing romance. Discovering the fantastic sisterhood of romance writers (both published and unpublished) in Britain and America made it a wild and wonderful journey to her first Mills & Boon® novel.

Heidi loves to hear from readers—you can e-mail her at **heidi@heidi-rice.com** or visit her website: www.heidi-rice.com

D1388631

Cupcakes and Killer Heels

Heidi Rice

First published in Great Britain 2011
by Mills & Boon, an imprint of Harlequin (UK) Limited,
Eton House, 18-24 Paradise Road, Richmond, Surrey TW9 1SR

© Heidi Rice 2011

ISBN: 978 0 263 88377 0

Harlequin (UK) policy is to use papers that are natural, renewable and recyclable products and made from wood grown in sustainable forests. The logging and manufacturing process conform to the legal environmental regulations of the country of origin.

Printed and bound in Spain
by Blackprint CPI, Barcelona

Also by Heidi Rice

Unfinished Business with the Duke
Public Affair, Secretly Expecting

Did you know these are also available as eBooks?
Visit www.millsandboon.co.uk

TM

For women who love chocolate and cupcakes
and can live with that extra inch on the thighs!
Like *moi*!

With special thanks to Lorraine
and the nice peeps at the Lincoln's Inn Library.

CHAPTER ONE

TAKE a chill pill, pal. This is a make-up emergency.

Pouting into her rear-view mirror, Ruby Delisantro tuned out the blare of a car horn from behind her and concentrated on applying a quick coat of Rose Blush Everstay lip gloss to calm jittery nerves.

She'd had the small but exclusive chain of Hampstead brasseries on her hit list for over a year. It had taken her months to get this afternoon's appointment with their chef and she wanted to look her absolute best before she started the long search for a parking space.

The squeal of brakes and the teeth-jarring jolt that followed was a little harder to ignore though—as it shot her forty-quid tube of Rose Blush straight up her nose.

'For Pete's sake!'

Extricating the lipstick from her left nostril

and hastily repairing the damage, she leapt out of her car. Having some bozo rear-end her was not the best way to prepare for her career-defining moment. Plus she'd just had Scarlett serviced and MOT'd at a cost of two hundred and twenty pounds. If any harm had been done to her beloved Bug, someone was going to die.

'Hey, hotshot. What's your problem? Don't you know where your brake pedal is?' she yelled at the man shielded behind the windscreen of the fancy Italian convertible pressed up against her bumper.

Typical. Only in Hampstead. A boy racer driving a lot more car than he can handle.

Gripping the top of the windscreen, Boy Racer jerked upright and jumped out of his car in one athletic movement. Ruby's lungs ceased to function and the fervent wish that she'd actually lost the six pounds she'd been debating losing for nearly a decade flitted through her mind.

This was no boy. This was most definitely a man.

A tall, strong, long-limbed, super-gorgeous man with close-cropped dark hair, broad shoulders and slim hips expertly displayed in worn, low-slung jeans. His eyes were disguised behind a pair of expensive sunglasses, but the manly dent in his chin and the shadow of stubble defining chiselled cheeks weren't doing a thing for Ruby's breathing difficulties, especially when his head dipped.

Is he checking me out?

'What's *my* problem?' He threw up his hands, making his muscular torso ripple under a T-shirt emblazoned with the slogan: 'Barristers do it on a trial basis.' 'What's *your* problem, lady? You're parked in the middle of the road.'

Ruby gulped in air to kick-start her lungs and took a moment to consider her response.

The good news was, Ruby Delisantro loved to flirt. And she was remarkably good at it. She adored the spark and sizzle of sexual attraction, the tantalising tension of verbal foreplay—and a chance to flirt with someone this good-looking didn't present itself every day. Not only that, but the figure-hugging dress she'd picked up at Camden Market last week turned the extra weight she'd been carrying around since she was seventeen into a major asset.

The bad news was, Mr Super-Gorgeous also had a super-large stick up his backside about women drivers and seemed to be virtually oblivious to her fabulous frock. Which meant he was either gay, a misogynist or didn't have a sense of humour. Any one of which should have been a major turn-off.

Unfortunately they weren't. Quite.

Hold it right there, Ruby.

She raised her gaze from her contemplation of his pectoral muscles. What was she thinking? She didn't have time to flirt with this guy—no matter how spectacular he might look in a dorky T-shirt. She had to see a man about some cupcakes.

'There was more than enough room to get past me,' she replied tartly, sending him a hard stare. 'And anyhow, it was an emergency.' *Sort of.*

The direction of his gaze dipped to her mouth. She mentally crossed 'gay' off her list as her tongue slid out to moisten lips that had suddenly turned to parchment.

No flirting, Ruby. This is non-negotiable.

He huffed out an incredulous laugh. 'Since when is putting lipstick on an emergency?'

'I had my parking lights on,' she continued, ignoring the jibe. Men were hard-wired not to understand the importance of lipstick, so she wasn't about to explain how the simple act of putting it on could bolster one's confidence in a business situation. 'And you ran into me.' She strutted towards him, grateful her four-inch heels went some way to correcting the height disadvantage.

Maybe she didn't have time to flirt. But she certainly had time to make him suffer.

'And if you had ever bothered to read your Highway Code,' she added, 'you'd know that puts you in the wrong. No matter how much testosterone you're packing.'

She flicked a contemptuous glance at his crotch to emphasise the point. Only to have her gaze snag on the prominent package displayed by the loose-fitting denims. A flush burned the back of her neck, stunning her even more—Ruby Delisantro was not and had never been a blusher.

He stepped forward—making her far too aware of exactly how tall he was.

'Those are hazard lights,' he said, the rich, masculine voice low and amused. 'Not parking lights.' He crossed his arms, making his biceps bunch under the short sleeves of his dorky T-shirt, and Ruby lost her train of thought completely.

'And if *you'd* bothered to read *your* Highway Code you'd know that,' he continued. 'No matter how much *oestrogen* you're packing.'

His head dipped again, the glint of August sunlight on the dark lenses of his shades doing nothing to disguise the fact that he was staring straight at her cleavage.

'And while I can see that's rather a lot,' he continued, a superior smile curving sensual lips, 'it's no excuse not to follow the rules of the road.'

Ruby's nipples puckered into hard points and the throb of something hot and uncomfortable swelled between her thighs. She resisted the urge to squirm. Barely.

Okay, this was just plain wrong. He was telling her off *and* turning her on at one and the same time. She might love to flirt, but she was not a masochist.

She slapped a hand on her hip.

'I don't do rules,' she purred, pointing a coral-tipped nail at the centre of his chest. A muscle in his jaw clenched and power surged through her. 'It makes life so dull, don't you think?'

She lifted her finger, satisfied she'd won, only to gasp when his hand shot out and long fingers clamped on her wrist. He pulled off his sunglasses, and she shivered involuntarily, stunned by the deep forest-green of his irises.

'Sounds to me like you need more than just driving lessons,' he murmured, the emerald stare so penetrating her thigh muscles turned to mush.

She tugged her hand free, hoping he hadn't felt her pulse hitting warp speed under his thumb. 'And like all men, I suppose you think you're man enough to teach me,' she scoffed. So what if she was playing with fire? She could see the heat smouldering in his eyes, making the rush of adrenaline so intoxicating it didn't leave much room for caution.

He gave a gruff chuckle. 'I'm not like other men,' he said softly, his confidence matching those come-to-bed eyes.

Ruby rubbed her wrist where the skin sizzled. 'That's what they all say.'

'No doubt,' he said, not sounding daunted. 'But I can prove it. The question is are you woman enough to let me?'

The husky invitation detonated the heavy weight already pulsing at her core.

Ruby blinked, and stepped back.

Whoa there, Ruby. Slow the hell down.

The situation had spiralled out of her control, and she wasn't sure how.

She might be an incurable flirt but she wasn't about to date a guy after knowing him for approximately ten seconds—even if he did have the uncanny ability to short-circuit her hormones.

Plus her sixth sense was yelling at her that this guy was nowhere near her type. Beneath those mouth-watering pecs and that sexy, laid-back self-confidence, Ruby detected a control that was unnervingly focused and intense.

She flicked her long curls of chestnut hair over her shoulder. 'What a tempting offer,' she said with as much sarcasm as she could muster. The guy's ego was enormous enough already. 'But I've already got a date this afternoon,' she said, ensuring her appointment with the chef at Cumberland sounded personal. 'And I don't do threesomes.'

The rich, resonant sound of his laughter rippled up her spine as she waltzed back to her car. She sashayed her hips—to make it clear this was a dignified retreat, and in no way a surrender.

'Pity,' he called after her. 'And there I was thinking you were a bad girl.'

She glanced at him as she opened the door. 'Wrong again,' she shot back, stifling the twinge of regret. Did he have to look quite so spectacular leaning against his sports car, the sun turning his short dark hair to a gleaming ebony and the challenge in those striking green eyes all but irresistible?

'I'm not a girl. I'm a woman.'

Callum Westmore laughed as the statuesque young beauty climbed back into her fire-engine red car. 'You got that right,' he murmured appreciatively.

The car suited her, he thought as it puttered to life. With its classy curves and bold, in-your-face style. He winced at the crunch of gears. And like its owner, it wasn't used to being driven.

As the car pulled away she flicked her hand out of the window in a flippant wave. He chuckled and sent her an equally flippant salute back. Not easy with the heat pulsing hard in his groin.

A slow grin split his features. And the heat pulsed harder.

Wasn't that a surprise?

When had he ever found a firebrand like her so tempting? And one who had given him the brush-off for no good reason. Because he'd bet a month's salary the date she'd mentioned didn't exist. He'd seen the way her glaze faltered—the classic tell for an unreliable witness.

His smile died as her car paused at the end of the leafy London lane, and he noticed the cracked brake light and the tilting bumper. The car turned onto Hampstead High Road and he read the words 'A Touch of Frosting: Bespoke Cupcakes', a web address and a telephone number written in glittering pink lettering on the door.

She disappeared into the traffic and he turned to examine the front of his own car, astonished to realise he'd been so distracted by their sparring match he hadn't checked to see if there was any damage to his treasured new Ferrari.

Luckily there was only a small scuff mark on the bumper. He rubbed it with his thumb, then climbed back into the car and retrieved his phone from the glove compartment.

However much he might have enjoyed arguing with the girl, the fender-bender had been primarily his fault. She might have been double parked, but he'd taken the corner too fast and run into her. And as she'd pointed out so provocatively, the Highway Code was fairly clear on the subject. He keyed her number into the phone.

Cal always played by the rules. The law wasn't just his profession, he demanded order and accountability in his personal life too. So he'd have to track the girl down and pay for the damage.

He squinted into the sun and put on his shades, the smile returning.

The thought of seeing her again wasn't exactly unappealing. He usually preferred the women he dated to be predictable and undemanding. Which made his instant attraction to The Lush Ms Reckless a bit disconcerting. The woman had high-maintenance written all over her—in mile-high neon letters.

But his social life had been non-existent ever since Gemma had called a halt to their occasional sleepovers a month ago—just because he'd refused point blank to let her move in. He liked his own space, his solitude, what was so hard to understand about that? With two high-profile cases lined up already for next month, he'd resigned himself to a celibate summer.

But now the thrill of the chase beckoned— and he had the whole of the August Bank Holiday weekend to play.

Cal tapped his thumb on the steering wheel, remembering the petal-soft skin on the inside of the girl's wrist, the frantic punch of her pulse and the way her brown eyes had melted to a molten chocolate. The live-wire attraction between them had been mutual. He was sure of it.

Cal's grin widened as he turned on the ignition. The smashed brake light and damaged bumper gave him the perfect excuse to tussle with Ms Reckless again. And next time she wouldn't be able to give him the brush-off so easily.

CHAPTER TWO

'How did it go?'

Ruby glanced up at her assistant Ella's eager enquiry as she flung her bag and the hefty file folder of product photos onto the brand new leather sofa in Touch of Frosting's freshly painted reception area.

She kicked off her heels and flopped onto the sofa.

'Don't ask,' Ruby moaned, propping her aching feet on the maplewood coffee table—which she'd splurged on a week ago along with the sofa and paint job, convinced she was going to secure the Cumberland order today.

Ella plopped down beside her. 'But I thought it was in the bag?'

'It would have been, if Scarlett's bumper hadn't fallen off and made me twenty minutes late for my appointment.' Ruby dropped her head against the sofa cushions and let out a heartfelt sigh. 'Unfortunately, chefs with two Michelin stars aren't known for their patience and understanding. Gregori Mallini refused to see me, then his sous chef gave me a ten-minute lecture about how precious the great Mallini's time is and informed me he didn't do business with people who couldn't bother to be prompt.'

'Oh, no.'

Ruby swivelled her head to see the sympathetic frown on Ella's face and the usual dusting of icing sugar on her nose and cheeks—and the tide of guilt almost swamped her. 'That would be the child-friendly way of putting it.'

Ella's frown deepened. 'But didn't you have Scarlett serviced, like, a week ago?'

'Yes…but that would be before she got hit on by a swanky Italian sports car.'

And my hormones led me astray with its equally swanky owner.

If only she hadn't got sidetracked by the guy, she would have noticed the damage to her car… Or at the very least given herself enough time to get to the precious appointment on time.

She wanted to kick herself. And she would have to, if her toes weren't screaming in agony after racing across half of Camden in the high-heeled shoes she'd bought specially to impress a chef she'd failed to actually meet.

'You were in an accident!' Ella gasped. 'Are you all right?'

'There's nothing to worry about,' Ruby said calmly, Ella's concern making the wave of guilt crest. Her partner in A Touch of Frosting was also her best friend. They'd been BFFs since nursery school. Ella was ditzy, impossibly sweet and a poet when it came to designing cupcake icing. She deserved better than this. 'I'm fine.'

Or at least she would be when she got over wanting to commit hara-kiri on one of her own kitchen knives. When was she going to start behaving like a grown-up—and stop getting distracted by every handsome guy that caught her eye? She'd been being so good lately, so why the heck had she picked today of all days to fall off the wagon?

Mr Swanky Italian Sports Car probably hadn't even been all that good-looking. She could see now she had probably exaggerated his appeal because of her nerves over the appointment at Cumberland and the shock of getting rear-ended and having her lipstick shoved up her nose.

Ruby frowned.

Damn.

And here she was obsessing about *him* again. A guy whose name she didn't even know. And who probably wasn't anywhere near as gorgeous as she remembered. When she'd promised herself she was going to stop doing that hours ago.

'Are you sure you're okay? You look really upset,' Ella murmured.

Ruby forced a tight smile onto her lips. 'If I'm upset it's only with myself.' She sighed again. 'I've let you down, El. I've let us both down. Getting Touch of Frosting cupcakes onto the afternoon tea menu at Cumberland's could have put us on the map. The orders would have come flooding in.' She gave a heavy sigh as she let the dream slip away once and for all.

Blast and double blast.

'We would have become the queens of cupcake design,' Ruby added, struggling to find some humour in the situation. 'A Nobel Prize for Baking would have been within our grasp at last.'

Ella grinned, her round pretty face lighting up as Ruby had intended. 'Just don't stop dreaming, Rubes. That's what you're good at.'

Shame I'm not as good at flirt control.

Ruby pushed the thought away and sat up.

Ella was right, there would be other opportunities. As long as they didn't stop dreaming big… And making the best damn cupcakes in the known universe. And beating herself up over Gregori high-and-mighty Mallini and the Cumberland order—and her flirt-control problems—wasn't going to get it done.

She'd just have to do better next time.

Standing up, Ella offered Ruby her hand. 'Come on,' she said, hoisting Ruby off the sofa with one swift tug. 'I've got something for you to taste. I think I've found the perfect frosting to complement your new mango-and-passion-fruit sponge base.'

Ruby felt the familiar flicker of excitement as she followed Ella, anticipating their latest culinary delight. Discovering a great new sponge-frosting combo was a lot more fun than contemplating her love life.

If only cupcakes could give her an orgasm—and she could flirt with them—her life would be perfect. She resolutely banished the image of Mr No-Name from her morning fender-bender and the thought that he might be the equivalent of the perfect cupcake in bed. No such man existed.

The usual swell of pride tightened Ruby's chest as she strolled into the kitchen she and Ella had mortgaged themselves to the hilt to buy the leasehold on two years before.

This was where she belonged. This was what mattered in her life. She adored the quick heady rush of falling in love, but she'd learned to her cost that it never lasted long— and then there was always the sticky business of falling back out of love again to handle. Love was fickle. It had certainly never been able to provide the same constancy or depth of satisfaction as her state-of-the-art catering kitchen. Tucked away in a Hampstead backstreet, the light, airy space with its utilitarian stainless steel surfaces and sink, the open shelves stacked with cake-baking equipment, the two top-of-the-range ovens, and its wardrobe-size cold room, probably wasn't most women's idea of bliss. But it was everything she wanted in her life. Because she and Ella had built it themselves from the ground up. And they got to call all the shots.

As long as she had her business, she was perfectly content to do without Mr Right. For the time being at least. Maybe one day she'd be ready to start searching for him, but she'd never been great at multitasking—as Johnny, her latest Mr Not Quite Right, had pointed out six months ago when they'd parted ways. She hadn't meant to hurt him, but she had. Being cast in the role of femme fatale wasn't high on her list of experiences to repeat any time soon, so she'd made a conscious decision not to get involved again for a while. And so far that was working out fine—give or take the odd hormone-induced blip, like this morning's.

Ella rushed ahead to the industrial-size mixing bowl and, scraping out a spatula of pale yellow buttercream icing, swirled it on the sponge samples Ruby had baked before she'd left for her appointment.

'Try that and tell me what you think,' Ella said, her voice reverent with hope, her eyes bright with anticipation.

The taste exploded on Ruby's tongue, spicy and citrusy and luxuriously fresh.

She hummed with pleasure. 'It's an over-used phrase, but that seriously is better than sex.' Or better than the vast majority of the sex she'd had.

Ella laughed and clapped her hands. 'It's good, isn't it?'

'It's not good, El. It's orgasmic. I can taste

orange and lemon and maybe a hint of cinnamon, but there's something else there. What is it?'

Ella touched her nose, her grin widening. 'That would be telling, but it took me two hours of sampling before I figured it out.'

'Well, it was worth it. We should add it to the menu right away. It'll be perfect for summer events. Let's debut it on the cupcake tower at Angelique Devereaux's wedding.' Ruby's mind raced with the logistics of getting the new recipe maximum exposure.

'Talking of love and orgasmic sex,' Ella interrupted, typically uninterested in the details that Ruby was so good at taking care of, 'I had a very nice chat with the new man in your life an hour ago.' Ella's grin turned cheeky. 'Why didn't you tell me you'd lifted your boyfriend embargo? If he looks half as good as that delicious voice sounds I'm guessing you hit the jackpot this time.'

'What new man?' Ruby said, her whirring mind grinding to a halt.

'Callum Westmore, that's who,' Ella replied easily, obviously still convinced Ruby was keeping secrets.

Ruby searched her inventory of names. She'd gone out with a few guys in the last six months, just to keep her hand in. But she hadn't agreed to a second date with any of them—always mindful of her new business-first-romance-last strategy. 'I don't know anyone called Callum.'

Ella's brow creased. 'Are you sure?'

'Of course I'm sure. I may be flighty but I always get a guy's name before I date him. It's fairly essential information,' she finished wryly.

Ella touched her fingers to her lips. 'Oops.'

'Why oops?' Ruby demanded. She didn't like the guilty look on Ella's face.

'I thought you were dating him. He sounded so confident and… Well, he had this amazing voice. A bit posh but not too posh and really deep and purposeful. And he said he needed to see you. Urgently. So I told him we finished at 5:30 p.m.'

'You gave him the address to the kitchen?' It was Ruby's turn to frown. She had a rule, which Ella was very well aware of, not to give casual dates her workplace info, because it only confused things. 'Oh, Ella, you didn't.'

And more importantly, who the heck was this guy? He certainly wouldn't be the first to try and get her details out of Ella. But no one had ever managed it before. Ella was usually a complete Rottweiler when it came to guarding Ruby's privacy—because she knew just how determined Ruby was to resist temptation, especially since the messy break-up with Johnny.

So how had Callum Westmore, whoever the heck he was, managed to wheedle the information out of Ella with such apparent ease?

The image of Mr Super-Gorgeous popped into her mind. The man she hadn't been able to get out of her head all afternoon. Despite all her best efforts.

'What exactly did this Callum Westmore say? In his sexy voice?' Ruby asked, but she was already fairly certain. He had to be the one. Who else did she know who would be arrogant and confident enough to ring up and brazenly muscle the information he wanted out of her best friend without breaking a sweat?

'Just that he needed to see you,' Ella said carefully. 'In fact, he sort of demanded to see you,' she added, as if the thought had only now occurred to her. 'But to be honest, it didn't even cross my mind to refuse him. He sounded so sure of himself.'

I'll just bet he did.

Ruby cursed softly under her breath.

Still, at least she had a name, now. Callum Westmore. It sounded like the name of a twelfth-century Scottish warlord. Which fitted him down to a T. Commanding, completely uncompromising and defiantly masculine— and prepared to swoop down and carry off any female who caught his fancy, whether she wanted him to or not.

The frisson of heat at the fanciful, romantic and utterly un-PC image stunned Ruby for a moment. Callum Westmore was about as far from her ideal date as it was possible to get. She should have found his pushy behaviour exceptionally galling. So why was her heart kicking giddily in her chest at the prospect of seeing him again?

The bright trill of the doorbell made them both jump.

She glanced at her watch. Five-thirty precisely.

'That's him,' she muttered. Trust him to be ridiculously prompt. Which was another good reason to dislike the man. Promptness was a skill she'd never quite managed to master herself—as this afternoon's fiasco with Gregori Mallini proved—and one she found slightly intimidating in other people.

'Do you want me to tell him you're not here?' Ella whispered, as if their uninvited guest could hear through walls.

Ruby considered the offer. For about a second.

'No. He's probably spotted my car.' And even if he hadn't, she somehow knew Callum Westmore would see straight through the ruse. Ella, with her open, uncomplicated nature and big doe eyes, couldn't lie worth a damn—and, anyway, Callum Westmore clearly wasn't the sort of guy who took no for an answer.

'Don't worry,' Ruby said, marching out of the kitchen. 'I'll handle this.'

She threw the words over her shoulder as she strode through the reception area to the front door of the business unit.

Okay, maybe her attraction to him was a little surprising…and ever so slightly disconcerting. But she had no doubt at all that she could handle Callum Westmore just fine.

He might have the name and the dominating masculinity of a twelfth-century Scottish warlord, but she was no simpering little virgin.

The prickle of irritation, though, was twinned with the heightened hum of arousal as she spied Westmore's tall frame silhouetted against the frosted glass of the door. She took a deep breath and turned the knob, secure in the knowledge that no man got to sweep Ruby Delisantro off her feet…

Not unless she wanted him to.

CHAPTER THREE

'MR WESTMORE, I presume,' Ruby remarked to broad shoulders—their width accentuated by the perfectly tailored jacket of a dark blue business suit—and the short-cropped hair on the back of his head.

She swallowed as he turned, and those heavy-lidded emerald-green eyes locked on her face.

Damn.

She should have taken the time to put her shoes back on. Without the benefit of the four-inch heels, she was at eye level with his chest, which, even clad in a white shirt and royal-blue silk tie instead of the bicep-hugging T-shirt of earlier in the day, still looked remarkably impressive. She jerked her eyes back to his face, in time to see a slow, distinctly knowing smile curve his lips.

He slung a hand into the pocket of his suit

trousers, disarming dimples appearing in his cheeks—which were now clean-shaven, but no less chiselled.

'Ms Delisantro, I presume,' he murmured, the husky tone making her pulse points throb.

Her breath escaped from her lungs in a rush.

Her imagination had not exaggerated his attractiveness, or that industrial-strength sex appeal, one bit. He really was Super-Gorgeous. Even in a suit. Which was saying something. She didn't usually go for the slick, executive type. She'd dated an accountant once and it had been a total disaster, his fastidious time-keeping and clinical attention to detail driving her batty within a week.

She concentrated on breathing evenly and getting her heart rate back under control. Somehow she doubted Callum Westmore was an accountant—or the fastidious type, despite the razor-sharp crease in his trousers. Maybe it was just that force field of raw machismo that radiated off him, but she couldn't imagine him bothering to crunch numbers.

'Now the introductions are done,' she said, trying not to sound too breathless, 'I'm intrigued to know what you're doing here.' She paused to think of an appropriate put-down. 'And why you saw fit to wheedle personal information out of my business partner.'

'I don't wheedle,' he said as his gaze glided over her figure. 'Even in extenuating circumstances.'

She resisted the urge to curl her toes, the painstakingly slow and thorough perusal making her feel as if it weren't just her feet that were naked.

His eyes lifted back to her face, the penetrating green alight with amusement. 'And I'd say why I'm here is fairly obvious.'

The suggestive comment and the gruff tone, thick with innuendo, made her feel warm all over, but she refused to fall for the ploy. She wasn't walking into that one. What did he think? That she was an amateur?

She cocked her head to one side, and let her gaze rake over him in return. Pursing her lips, she sent him a deliberately quizzical look, pleased when his eyes flicked to her mouth. 'I guess it's not as obvious as you thought, because I can't think of a single reason.'

He chuckled, acknowledging the hit with an unsettling lack of concern. 'Why don't I spell it out, then, Ms Delisantro?' he said, lingering on her name. 'So you can stop worrying about it.'

'I'm not worried,' she said, emphatically. 'Just mildly curious.'

He raised one dark brow. 'Only mildly?'

He had her there—given that she was about to spontaneously combust with a lot more than mild curiosity. 'That's right,' she lied.

'I see.' The assured smile made it obvious he wasn't fooled. 'Well, happily I'm willing to satisfy your mild curiosity.' He put the emphasis on satisfy and her whole body began to throb. 'But only if you're willing to satisfy me first.'

Why did she have the feeling they weren't talking about curiosity any more, mild or otherwise? And why couldn't she resist the challenge in those smoky green eyes?

'What do you want, Mr Westmore?' she said boldly, rising to the bait he had so purposefully dangled in front of her.

'I'd like to get to know you better.' His eyes flashed, the predatory gleam triumphant. 'A lot better.'

She'd been expecting the invitation. Had been prepared to turn him down—and put him in his place. But the words refused to come out of her mouth.

'So that's why you went to all the trouble of tracking me down,' she replied, putting just the right amount of indifference into her tone. 'To ask me on a date?' She battered her eyelashes. 'I suppose I should be flattered.'

He didn't seem fazed by the put-down. If anything, he looked more assured than ever. Drat the man.

'Actually, that's not the primary reason why I phoned and spoke to your partner.'

'Don't forget the wheedling,' Ruby added cheekily, enjoying the sizzle as his eyes narrowed.

Sparring with this man had an edge of danger that only made it more irresistible. Which was definitely a bad thing. But she was finding it hard to care. She'd had a monumentally crappy day—and he was partially responsible. It seemed only reasonable she should allow herself a moment to flirt with him, as a consolation.

'As I said, Ms Delisantro, I don't wheedle. That was the fine art of persuasion.'

Ruby shrugged, admiring his dimples. He was definitely more dangerous when he smiled. 'So what was the primary reason you tracked me down, then? And wheedled?'

The dimples deepened. 'I came to pay for the damage to your car.'

She was so surprised, the statement left her momentarily lost for words. 'You're joking?'

'I caused the damage, I pay. Those are the rules,' he said, as if that kind of gallantry were the norm.

'Don't you ever break the rules?' she asked.

'Never.'

'That's fortunate,' she murmured, astonished to find his conformity as sexy as the rest of him.

She wasn't big on rules and regulations herself. As long as she wasn't hurting anyone, where was the harm in bending them a bit? And she'd always been drawn to men with the same free and easy attitude.

She would never break the law, not since she'd been egged into shoplifting at the tender age of twelve by a boy she'd idolised. The guilt had eaten at her for days, until she'd finally told her father. He'd marched her down to apologise to the shopkeeper in question and pay for the candy necklace she'd taken. The shame had nearly killed her, and she'd promised herself she'd never do anything illegal again.

But that didn't mean she wasn't prepared to question the status quo—whenever necessary. If a boundary was presented to her, she felt honour-bound to push at it. She suspected Callum Westmore's code of ethics was so unyielding, he would insist on pushing back.

But since when had she found that sort of rigidity appealing?

'On the contrary,' he said, his deep green eyes glinting at her. 'That's civilisation.'

Funny, that gleam in his eyes wasn't what she'd call civilised.

His gaze dipped to her feet. 'Put some shoes on, and we'll discuss how much I owe you over dinner.'

She bristled at the dictatorial tone. The man was far too used to ordering women around. But she decided not to challenge him. Yet. The thought of spending the evening with him, the sexual energy humming between them, was tantalising. Especially as she already knew their date couldn't possibly lead anywhere. This guy was so not her type, on so many levels. And spending the evening with him would make that blatantly obvious.

'I'll go to dinner with you on one condition,' she said, deciding to test his limits. 'I get to pick the venue.'

Her friend Sol's Cuban bar on Camden Lock hosted a salsa evening on Friday night. It was a popular hang-out for her and her wide circle of friends and neither the fiery tapas nor the dance moves were for the faint-hearted.

Westmore would feel instantly uncomfortable in the Bohemian surroundings in his suit and tie and she doubted he'd have the guts to brave the dance floor, no matter how arrogant he was. She almost felt sorry for him. But seeing him struggle to fit in at Sol's would be a quick fix for the bizarre effect he had on her. And she'd be able to blow him off at the end of the evening without a single regret. Plus Dave, her mechanic, had already quoted her two hundred pounds for the repairs to Scarlett and the offer Westmore had made, which would mean she didn't have to dig into her no claims bonus, wasn't something she could afford to pass up.

He nodded, completely oblivious to his impending ordeal. 'As long as the food's edible and I'm footing the bill, I don't have a problem with that.'

As Ruby went to get her shoes and repair her make-up she felt the tiny stab of guilt. Normally she insisted on going Dutch on a first date, so the guy didn't get the wrong idea,

and making the man pay for his own humiliation seemed a bit mean. But as she left Ella to
lock up, and stepped out into the early evening
sunshine to see Callum Westmore leaning
against the gleaming black paintwork of his
pricey Italian convertible, confidence oozing
from every pore, the guilt turned to anticipation and the pleasant hum of arousal peaked.
The man needed to have his ego taken down
a peg or two, and her body needed a wake-up
call. And she'd found the perfect way to do
both.

Once tonight was over, the all-conquering
Callum Westmore would have discovered that
not every woman who fancied him was prepared to fall at his feet.

The minute they walked into the bustling bar
tucked away on the canal path at the bottom
of Camden Market, Cal knew exactly what
Ruby's game was.

Her hourglass figure moved enticingly in
the fifties-style cotton dress as she waved to
the barman and shouted a greeting. A swarthy
youth in his early twenties rushed over and
directed them to a secluded table on the other
side of the dance floor—while slanting Cal an
assessing stare.

Cal pressed his palm to the warm bare skin of Ruby's back to guide her through the crowded tables and felt the slight jolt she couldn't disguise. A smile edged his lips as he caught the waiter's glare before the younger man hurried away.

The crowd were young and trendy, the music from a band in the corner loud and vibrant and the smell of fresh sweat and exotic spices all but overwhelming. Couples followed the intricate steps of the salsa with easy grace on a terrace overlooking the canal, their lithe young bodies entwined as they moved in time with the throbbing bongo beat that accompanied the blatantly sexual dance. At barely six o'clock, the place was already packed. One of the waitresses, hefting a tray laden with tapas dishes and bottles of Mexican beer, stopped to give Ruby a quick kiss and then grinned and whispered something in her ear while giving Cal a deliberate once-over. By the time they'd reached their table, they'd been stopped a dozen times, with Ruby shouting introductions over the blare of the music and voices, her face glowing with a potent blend of expectation, excitement and casual confidence.

Shrugging off his jacket, he draped it over the chair, then pulled off his tie and slipped it in his pocket. Undoing the top buttons of his shirt, Cal made himself comfortable, more than ready to take whatever Ms Ruby Delisantro had to throw at him.

She'd planned to show him up by bringing him here, that much was obvious. No doubt expecting him to be some boring suit who would balk at the idea of getting down and dirty at a neighbourhood bar where she was the queen bee. The ploy made him smile.

Unfortunately for her, she'd miscalculated. He didn't give in that easily. He wasn't the snob or the killjoy she'd obviously mistaken him for. And he happened to enjoy dancing, especially when it was with a beautiful woman whom he'd been desperate to get his hands on all day. Latin dancing in particular could be a very satisfying form of foreplay, especially when you knew the steps—and he had a feeling Ruby knew this dance very well indeed. What she didn't know was that so did he.

He settled in his chair and waited for her to finish chatting with yet another friend who had crossed the bar to greet her. He stiffened then forced himself to relax when the young man grabbed her round the waist and hauled her up for a quick kiss. He suspected Ruby's bright, breezy, social-butterfly act was for his benefit so he should sit back and enjoy the show.

She wriggled out of the guy's arms and gave him a jaunty pat on the cheek, making it subtly clear with her body language that, while she enjoyed the attention, their friendship was purely platonic. The guy gave him a brief nod as Ruby introduced them, then wound his way through the crowd, obviously used to getting the brush off.

Boy, but she was good. A natural flirt, who had the ability to make guys feel great without leading them on.

He'd hazard a guess that Ruby Delisantro only chose to date men who let her dictate all the moves. And he guessed she'd have no shortage of willing candidates mesmerised by that voluptuous body, her boldly beautiful face and her vibrant personality.

But that was before she'd met him.

He stretched out his legs, relishing the battle of wills ahead.

When was the last time he'd had to actively seduce a woman? To put some effort into the chase?

He'd chosen Gemma and nearly all of her predecessors in his bed, specifically because they'd been willing to let him set the pace.

What he hadn't realised until today was that his decision to always take the path of least resistance had resulted in his sex life becoming remarkably dull.

What was it they said about no pain, no gain?

He had the feeling Ruby, with her impulsive, flirtatious nature, her smart mouth and her desire to be in charge, had the potential to be a royal pain in the backside, but those very same qualities also made her electrifyingly sexy and a major challenge. And if the arousal flooding through his veins at the glimpse of cleavage as she propped her elbows on their table was anything to go by, the gain was going to be worth the pain.

Slinging his arm over the back of her chair, he leaned in close and brushed the unruly curls of hair behind her ear.

'Nice choice,' he murmured, loving the way she shivered as his breath brushed her ear lobe. 'Why don't you order for us? You seem to have the connections to get the best service and I'm famished.' She probably knew the menu off by heart. 'And then we can dance it off before we discuss damages.'

Her big brown eyes widened beautifully as

her head whipped round. 'You know how to salsa?'

'You'll have to wait and see,' he said, stroking the back of her neck with his thumb under the heavy fall of hair. 'But I think you'll discover I have a few talents.'

Salsa being the least of them.

She shivered again—and he had to resist the urge to throw back his head and laugh at the sparkle of irritation in her eyes and the dark sheen of stunned arousal.

Score one to me.

For goodness' sake.

The infernal man didn't look uncomfortable in the least. If anything, he looked positively smug. And if that weren't bad enough, the light rub of his thumb against her nape was making her want to roll over and purr. Pulling away from the sensual torture before she did just that, Ruby signalled Sol's wife, Chantelle, and ordered a selection of tapas dishes and a margarita for herself. Westmore then chimed in and ordered a beer—in fluent Spanish. Chantelle carried on a brief conversation with him of which Ruby only managed to catch about two words. Giving a throaty laugh, the waitress leaned over to clear the empty plates and glasses that had been left on their table and whispered in Ruby's ear.

'He's a hot one, *querida*,' she said in her thick Spanish accent, the tone husky with humour. 'Maybe even too hot for you to handle, eh?'

As Chantelle strolled off, the tray perched expertly on her arm, Ruby assessed her date. And struggled to regroup.

Well, he was certainly hot.

With his sleeves rolled up, her eyes were drawn to the muscles in his forearm as he tapped his fingers on the table to the beat of the music. Acknowledging the twist and throb of desire, she dismissed it.

So what if he was hot? He couldn't possibly be too hot for her to handle.

'Where did you learn to speak Spanish?' she asked. Maybe polite conversation was the best way to cool things down a bit. She liked heat as much as the next girl but getting incinerated wasn't part of her plan.

'I lived in Barcelona for a few years after law school.'

'You're a lawyer?' Which would explain his affinity for the rule of law, Ruby thought. But not her overwhelming attraction.

'I'm a barrister,' he corrected easily.

She could just picture him in court, directing a jury in robes and a white wig. Instead of making him seem ridiculous, the image only made him seem more commanding.

'And you make cupcakes for a living?' he countered.

'I do.' She straightened, waiting for the derogatory comment. People often thought what she did was frivolous and inconsequential. Given the gravity of this guy's profession, she could just imagine what he was thinking about her little bakery business.

'And according to the *Standard*, they're the best cupcakes in the known universe.'

'You read Ed Moulder's review?' The veteran food writer had gushed about A Touch of Frosting, and Ruby was inordinately proud of the review, but still the admiration in Callum's voice took her by surprise.

'The man had quite a crush on your cupcakes,' he added. 'And he's notoriously hard to please.'

'My cupcakes can be very seductive,' she said, her pleasure at the unexpected praise making her purr after all.

'I can well imagine.' His eyes darkened as he picked her hand up from the table, and turned it over. The hum of voices, the defiant throb of music seemed to fade away, until all she could hear was the hammer of her own heartbeat and the low murmur of his voice, whispering across her sensitised skin. 'But the question is, do they taste as good as you?'

She watched transfixed as he raised her hand to his mouth and bit softly into the pad of flesh on the base of her thumb. The shot of heat pounded into her breasts making them peak painfully against her push-up bra.

The breath lodged in her throat.

The line was corny, cheesy even—and from the mocking twist of his lips she guessed he knew it. But she was struggling to breathe, so scoffing was out of the question.

The sound of the bar came flooding back as Chantelle's arrival broke the spell. Her friend laid out their order on the table, then shot Ruby a teasing wink. Studiously ignoring the rush of blood to her cheeks, Ruby took a hasty sip of her margarita as her friend strolled off. The sweet icy tang of citrus, triple sec and tequila felt like nectar as it slid down her raw throat.

Cal saluted her with the frosty bottle of lager before bringing it to his lips. Her gaze landed on the strong column of his throat as he swallowed and she began to feel light-headed.

Holy moley. He is *too hot to handle.*

Unfortunately, just looking at those long fingers gripping the neck of the bottle and the sheen of sweat on his Adam's apple was making her feel euphoric. And more aroused than she had been in months. She'd been so careful lately, so cautious. But as the pounding salsa beat throbbed through her veins and she watched Cal drink thirstily Ruby felt her inhibitions float up and fly off across the Lock into the sultry summer night.

What the heck? She didn't intend to fall at his feet, but surely there was no harm in having fun for one night. It had been so long since she'd had the chance to indulge her inner flirt to the full. And frankly, Callum Westmore came in such a mouth-watering package, he was fast becoming too hot not to handle.

CHAPTER FOUR

'RUBY, are you trying to lead again?' Callum teased, his breath making her earlobe tingle. 'Because I may have to show you who's boss.'

'I'd like to see you try,' Ruby quipped, then laughed and clung on as he swung her round.

His answering chuckle made her head spin as he dipped her over his arm for one tantalising second. 'Consider yourself shown.'

She inhaled a lung full of the woody scent of his soap masked by the hint of fresh male sweat—and basked in the sultry rhythm of the salsa as he whisked her upright. His arm banded around her waist so tight she could feel every single inch of his hard, lean physique.

He was a good dancer. An exceptionally good dancer. Not only did he know the steps, but he moved with a fluid, natural grace unencumbered by his height, throwing her into the spins and dips with masterful strength and confidence.

Unfortunately, after two margaritas, only a nibble of the spicy tapas dishes and an hour of full-on flirting, Ruby was finding it impossible to concentrate on the dance, instead of all the parts of her body that were throbbing with need.

The desire to feel those hard, callused fingers on her naked skin—to lick the divot of his throat and taste the salty aroma of his sweat—overwhelmed her and her intoxication had nothing to do with the heady cocktails or the lack of food.

A small voice in her head kept telling her that he'd engineered this, that he'd been stoking the need all evening. Making her feel like the only woman in the bar with those long penetrating looks; tempting her as his gaze flicked to her mouth every time she licked dry lips; goading her as they vied for top spot in a seductive game of one-upmanship.

And now he was sealing his conquest in time-honoured tradition by holding her body close and leading her in a sensual dance of challenge and retreat. Promise and provocation.

But the more she breathed in his scent; the more she felt the muscles bunch beneath the fine cotton of his shirt; the more the husky tone of his voice played havoc with her senses; the quieter that dissenting voice became. Until all she could hear, roaring through every cell of her overwrought body, was the voice yelling, 'Go for it, Ruby.'

She'd never had a one-night stand before. Had always thought the concept highly overrated. Why would you want to share that kind of intimacy with a man you didn't know? And who didn't know you? But suddenly the glorious anonymity of one night of passion held a giddy thrill that was impossible to resist.

She'd sworn off relationships for the time being, but surely one night of indulgence didn't count.

And if you were going to have a one-night stand, who better to have it with than someone who had the sex appeal of Casanova—and about half as much depth?

She wouldn't be able to hurt a man like Callum Westmore, even if she tried.

The music slowed to a stop and Cal's hand rode down to rest on her hip. Her legs straddled one hard thigh, forcing her to press against the muscled sinew. Her eyes fixed on his lips and she noticed the shadow of stubble on his cheeks.

He swore softly, then clasped her head, and captured her mouth.

The contact was electric. His lips firm and warm. The insistent throbbing between her legs exploded as he deepened the kiss. She opened to accept the invasion, the strong sure strokes of his tongue leaving her breathless as he drew back.

'Let's get out of here,' he said, his gaze shuttered, his voice rough with lust. 'I don't do sex as a spectator sport.'

Yes, please.

Her mind screamed the words, but she could only nod, mute with longing, her lips still burning from the intensity of his kiss.

Damn it, he was about to explode.

Cal's hand squeezed Ruby's as he hauled her through the bar determined not to let her loose for a second. What had been fun at first, the exhilarating foreplay of flirt and counter-flirt, had turned to a torturous need that was about to send him hurtling over the edge into insanity if he didn't get her naked really, really soon.

Grabbing his jacket up from the chair, he

pulled out his wallet and threw a bunch of twenty-pound notes on the table.

'It won't be that much!' Ruby said as he clasped her hand and led her through the crowd to the exit.

He looked over his shoulder at her flushed face, the lips red where he'd all but devoured her on the dance floor. 'You want to wait for the change?'

She gave it a moment's thought, before her full lips spread into a smile. 'Chantelle's going to get extremely lucky tonight.'

He laughed, the sound strained. 'I certainly hope she's not the only one.'

The still evening air did nothing to quell the heat as he showed Ruby to his car. 'Where do you live?' he asked as he yanked open the passenger door.

'Tufnell Park.'

He slammed the door, then skirted the car and leapt into the driver's seat. Firing the engine, he shifted into gear.

'I live on the south end of the Heath.' The powerful hum of the engine was nothing compared to the driving need in his gut as he roared away from the kerb, then had to brake at the traffic lights on Camden High Road. He glanced at his passenger, fisting his fingers on the steering wheel. 'My place is closer.'

The smile got bigger. 'Excellent point.'

Leaning across the steering wheel, he plunged his fingers into her hair and hauled her close—unable to wait another moment to taste her again.

Her lips softened, her tongue tangling with his as he claimed her mouth.

The blast of a car horn forced him to release her as every last ounce of blood surged south. 'My place it is, then.'

She nodded, looking as dazed as he felt.

He stamped his foot on the accelerator. The screech of burning rubber as they shot away from the intersection made him jerk his foot off the pedal.

Get a grip, Westmore. It's sex. Not life or death.

He eased out a breath, holding his car under the speed limit as he made the series of turns through the backstreets of Hampstead then drove up the hill past the Heath.

By the time they reached the Victorian mansion block, he'd managed to get his breathing back under control, just about. He adjusted his trousers as he climbed out of the car to ease the pressure. Ruby stepped out the other side, her lush breasts pressing against the thin bodice of her dress. He extended his hand, but, instead of taking it, she clasped her bag to her midriff and a flicker of uncertainty crossed her face.

'Is there a problem?' he asked, more curtly than intended.

If she changed her mind now, it would probably cause him a serious injury.

She cleared her throat. 'Two things.' She clutched her bag tighter. 'Firstly, I don't have protection with me tonight. I wasn't expecting this.'

The relief that coursed through him almost made his knees give way. He locked them. 'I have protection,' he said. He would have used condoms anyway, he always did. But he had to give her points for foresight and practicality, especially as he knew she was as blindsided by lust as he was if her shallow pants were anything to go by. 'What's the other thing?'

'This feels a bit rushed,' she said, her voice trembling. 'And rushed doesn't really work for me.'

'I beg your pardon?' Clearly the loss of blood to his head had damaged his brain cells because he didn't have a clue what she was talking about.

She huffed. 'We're obviously very attracted to each other.'

Great, so what the hell is the problem?

'Agreed,' he said, damping down on his frustration. Whatever the problem was, it would be better to let her say it. He wasn't going to risk scaring her off.

'But I've never done this before.'

The bold statement, delivered with obvious bravado, made him feel even more clueless. He frowned, his frustration all but strangling him.

'What exactly is *this*?' he asked carefully. If she was about to tell him she was a virgin, he was going to be exceptionally annoyed with himself. How could his radar have been so spectacularly off?

'*This* is a one-night stand. I usually date a guy for a while before I consider going to bed with him.'

Relief coursed through him. Relief and something else, which he decided not to examine. So she didn't jump into bed with every guy who took her fancy. So what? Why should her sexual history matter to him? He'd always considered the double standard when it came to sex completely illogical. If a guy wanted a woman and acted on it, he certainly shouldn't hold it against her if she did the same.

'So what's your point?' he asked. And wished like hell she'd hurry up and get to it.

'The point is…' she began, her gaze darting away from his.

Finally.

'I'm not the sort of woman who has spontaneous orgasms to order.' She rushed the words as she met his gaze, her lips flattening into a firm line and her cheeks flushing a becoming shade of pink. 'So I'd appreciate it if you didn't rush things,' she finished.

His lips twitched at the defiant tone.

She was actually serious. The guys she'd dated had to be idiots.

He tried to keep a good firm grip on the amusement tightening his chest. Honestly, he did.

Maybe it was the extreme sexual frustration that made him lose it, or more likely the sight of her full lips pouting adorably as she laid down the law about how she expected to be made love to… But whatever it was, he was powerless to stop the rumble of laughter rising up and bursting out of his mouth.

'What's so funny?' she said, her voice ripe with exasperation.

He grasped her wrist, hauled her into his arms. 'Why don't I take it from here, Ruby?' He continued to chuckle as she struggled against him.

'You see, this is exactly the problem,' she said, her eyes flashing, her indignation not abating one bit. 'You don't know me and yet you're assuming…'

He silenced her with a kiss. Hunger quickly overwhelmed the hilarity, and she stopped wriggling. So he took his time. Hearing the sharp intake of breath as he traced her lips with the tip of his tongue. Revelling in her soft little moan as he nipped her plump bottom lip. He explored in slow, determined strokes. Breathing in her scent, he tasted the delicious mix of lemon and vanilla—a cocktail of flavours that were both sweet and intoxicating. His erection swelled painfully as she writhed in his arms, her fingers threading into his hair and her tongue duelling with his in a sensual dance that made him ache.

He cradled her face in his palms as he touched his forehead to hers, listened to her ragged breathing.

'I'm not going to rush you,' he murmured,

the humour gone. 'I've been waiting to get my hands on you the whole damn day. So believe me, I intend to savour every single second.'

His lips quirked as he lifted his head and took in her dilated pupils—and the little crease of consternation on her forehead.

'I know what I'm doing,' he added.

'Yes, but you don't—'

'And I don't need instructions,' he interrupted, grinning. Damn, but she was persistent. 'I find it ruins the spontaneity.'

She moved out of his arms, propped her hands on her hips, the little crease turning into the Grand Canyon. 'I should have guessed you'd be difficult about—'

'That's enough talk.'

'Excuse me?'

Stepping forward, he whipped her bag out of her hand.

'Hey, give that back.'

Ignoring the astonished protest, he grasped her wrist with his other hand, bent over and hefted her onto his shoulder.

'What are you doing?' she yelped, although he figured it was fairly obvious as he marched to the front door of his block.

'I like talk as much as the next guy,' he said conversationally as he keyed his code into the security panel. 'In fact, I make a very decent living at it.' He kicked open the door. 'But even I have my limits.'

'Put me down!' she yelled, wriggling and kicking now as she got her wind back. 'This is absurd.'

He elbowed the light switch.

'And probably illegal.' The protest came out in pants, her midriff rocking against his shoulder blade. 'I'll sue.'

Adrenaline surged through him as he climbed the stairs, two at a time.

'Go ahead and try.' He dropped her to her feet—and chuckled at her mutinous expression, and the flush of arousal on her cheeks. 'No judge would convict me.'

Her chin took on a mulish tilt, her colour rising. 'She would if she was a woman.'

'Wanna bet?' He reached into his pocket, palmed his key and slid it into the lock. Opening the door, he took hold of her hand and pulled her inside.

'Has anyone ever told you you're remarkably arrogant?' she announced as he slapped his palms above her head, caging her against the wall.

'Yes. You.' He buried his face against her neck. 'And more than once now.'

Her quickened breathing gushed out against his cheek. His lips at her pulse point, he heard the soft sob of surrender. He lifted his head, traced his fingers along the elegant line of her neck, over her collarbone, then ran his hands down her curves. She bucked, her body quaking as his thumbs circled the tight buds of her breasts through her clothing.

'And you're remarkably bossy,' he murmured, his hands settling on her hips. Why did he find that so incredibly sexy?

Her big brown eyes widened as he pushed his body hard against hers. 'Which makes us even.' Capturing her wrist, he led her down the hallway towards his bedroom.

Her heels clicked on the polished wood floor as she raced to keep pace with him. But for once she didn't have a comeback—which made him feel invincible.

CHAPTER FIVE

RUBY had never been so grossly manhandled in her entire life. Unfortunately, she'd never been so turned on, either.

Had he actually carried her up the stairs? Like Rhett Butler to her Scarlett O'Hara?

Of course, she didn't find his domineering behaviour romantic in the least—because it wasn't, in the slightest, she told herself staunchly. But there was definitely something exhilarating about a guy who could heft her up two flights of stairs. After all, she wasn't exactly light as a feather.

And then there was the feel of him to consider, pressing against her belly as he gave her one of the biggest love bites of her life. She was so excited, her pulse points weren't just throbbing any more, they were dancing a jig. And her nipples were so erect she could probably drill for oil with them.

As he propelled her into the bedroom she took in the terraced doors that opened onto a wrought-iron balcony overlooking the Heath. But she barely had a chance to register the dying sun turning the trees on Parliament Hill a brilliant orange before the hiss of her zipper had her whipping round.

She clasped her sagging bodice to her chest. 'Now wait a minute!'

Oblivious to her outrage, he placed a finger on her shoulder, and gave a gentle shove. The backs of her knees hit the bed, and she toppled unceremoniously onto the pale blue duvet. She scrambled up, abandoning her grip on the bodice, which promptly fell to her waist revealing her red lace bra.

'I told you, I don't like to be rushed.' She heaved out a breath, her insides going molten at the wicked glint in his eye as he knelt on the bed.

One strong hand clamped around her ankle.

'Who said anything about rushing?' The rough murmur vibrated across her nerve-endings as his hand tightened.

Slipping off her shoe, he flung it over his shoulder. Then dug his thumb into the tight muscles of her instep. She groaned, her body bowing back, as heat shimmered up her calf and made her thigh muscles quiver. He massaged with strong fingers until the muscles went liquid, then transferred his attention to the other foot.

Her heart lurched into her throat as he lifted her foot to his lips, those emerald eyes locked on her face, and bit into the arch.

She gasped, astonished to realise he was discovering erogenous zones she hadn't known existed as his callused fingers trailed up her legs, stroking and caressing with purpose. Butterfly kisses followed in their wake, distracting her as he hooked his fingers into the waistband of her panties.

She raised her bottom as he drew the scarlet lace down, welcoming the slight breeze from the terrace as he lifted the hem of her dress, bunching the skirt round her waist. She glanced down, and realised on a surge of horrified excitement that she was completely exposed to him.

'What are you doing?' She shuddered, so breathless, her lungs felt as if they were about to explode.

He looked up, the deep green dark with appreciation. 'Savouring you, remember.'

'But you can't... I'm not...' Her protest got

lodged in her throat when his tongue swirled across the inside of her thigh. She didn't even recognise the low, guttural moan of longing that echoed in her ears as her own. Her head dropped back on the pillow as she surrendered to the delicious torture of his open-mouthed caress.

'That's a good girl.' The satisfied chuckle should have annoyed her, but she couldn't think, let alone protest as his tongue licked and delved, in tortuously slow circles, taking an eternity to get closer and closer to the centre of ecstasy.

He grasped her hips, holding her open to him as her whole body quaked beneath the onslaught of his lips, his tongue, his teeth—poised on the edge of oblivion.

'Please…' she begged, the plea raw with desperation, not caring any more who was in charge, who had control, as long as he didn't stop.

Then, at last, he teased out the swollen nub and placed his lips on it. The pleasure built with staggering speed as her whimpers of need cut through the muggy silence.

She strained towards that glorious oblivion, so tantalisingly close and yet out of reach.

'Can you…?' She began, but her directions

cut off when one long, blunt finger entered her, his mouth still feasting on her swollen clitoris.

His finger stretched her, then pressed, twisting until he touched a spot deep inside and caressed. The monumental release triggered, sweeping through her like a firestorm.

Ruby shrieked, arching off the bed, the waves of orgasm shattering her into a billion glittering pieces.

'So you're a screamer.'

Ruby blinked as he propped his elbow beside her head and stared down at her.

'Good to know,' he added, looking smug, but she was still far too stunned to utter a single word, let alone respond to his teasing.

What had he done to her?

She'd never had an orgasm that intense before. Not even close. And she'd certainly never been a screamer. Until now.

'I like to show my appreciation,' she murmured, getting enough of her faculties back to know it would not be wise to mention he was the first man to hit that particular jackpot. He was looking far too pleased with himself already.

'Duly noted,' he quipped, placing a light kiss on her nose.

His gaze roamed over her and she struggled to control the desire to cover herself. Her mortification was complete when a blush fanned out across her chest.

How much more exposed could she be? She was sprawled on his bed, her half-naked body still flushed with afterglow, having had the most titanic orgasm of her life. And she hadn't had to give him a single instruction. Plus, she was pretty sure she'd begged.

He dipped his thumb under the thin lace of her bra, and her nipple tightened to his touch. His eyes locked back on her face as he delved behind her back.

'Let's get you naked,' he murmured.

She heard the sharp click as he unhooked her bra with one hand and then pulled the garment free, the slow seductive smile ripe with suggestion.

'You're gorgeous,' he muttered, cupping her breasts and then licking at the tip.

She thrust her fingers into his short silky hair, shocked to feel the renewed bolt of heat arrowing down to her core and the strange tug of emotion beneath her breastbone.

'I want you naked too,' she managed to

moan, the rasp of his stubble on tender flesh
sending her senses reeling.

He lifted his head, grinned. 'That's one instruction I'm happy to obey.'

Sitting up, he tugged his shirt over his head
with undisguised haste, the buttons popping.

Ruby took the opportunity to scramble out
of her dress as he grappled with his belt.

She'd analyse all this later. Her unprecedented response to him had to be a fluke
of chemistry—and the result of his considerable proficiency in the bedroom. The man had
said he was talented. He hadn't lied.

But then the mattress dipped as he knelt on
the bed beside her, and her gaze devoured the
lean musculature of his torso. He was even
more gorgeous naked if that were possible.
The slight sprinkle of hair defined well-devel-
oped pecs and bisected an awesome six-pack.
He must work out. A lot. Her gaze followed
the arrow down and then stopped dead. The
unfamiliar blush burned across her cheeks
like wildfire.

Oh, my goodness.

The massive erection stood out proudly
from the thatch of dark hair at his groin as
she watched him sheath himself. Her jaw went
slack. While she was coming to appreciate

Callum Westmore's talents, she hadn't expected him to be quite that talented.

'Wow,' she said, before she could think better of it.

The deep rumble of laughter sounded both self-satisfied and amused—and she realised she'd given him the upper hand. Again.

Holding her waist, he shifted her neatly beneath him. 'I'm glad you approve.'

She braced her hands on his chest, felt the muscles quiver like a stallion ready to mate. 'No need to look so full of it,' she quipped, trying to regain ground while her sex ached with need. 'Don't you know size doesn't matter?'

He chuckled, brushed her hair back from her face, then nipped her ear lobe, sending a shaft of heat to her core. 'Luckily for us both, then,' he whispered, 'I also know exactly what I'm doing.'

She couldn't help it, she giggled, the audacious comment making her abdomen tremble with anticipation.

I'll just bet you do.

Her fingers caressed the bunched muscles of his shoulder blades and fisted in the short hair at his nape.

'Talk is cheap, Westmore,' she teased,

pulling him down. The comforting weight of him anchored her to the mattress. 'Where's the proof?'

He didn't need to be asked twice.

She panted, sobbed, adjusting to the aching fullness as he lodged deep inside her in one long, solid thrust.

Establishing a rhythm, he forced her to take the full measure of him. She wrapped her legs round his waist, held on to sweat-slicked shoulders as she moved with him. His answering grunts rasped in her ears as the brutal heat eddied up from her toes, shimmering through her body and washing over her in ever growing waves of pleasure so intense she fought to hold them back—clinging to the wild need to make him shatter first.

He shifted suddenly, pressed one hot palm to her midriff, then found her clitoris with seeking fingers.

'No, don't,' she cried. But it was too late. His knowing fingers triggered the wild cry of release as another mind-blowing orgasm slammed into her with the force of a fist.

She could barely hear his harsh shout as he crashed over the same brutal edge a few seconds later.

* * *

Cal braced himself on unsteady arms and drew out, groaning as her body released him. He rolled onto his back, grateful that he'd managed to avoid collapsing on top of her.

That had been incredible. He cursed under his breath. Not incredible, more like mind-altering.

He twisted round to stare at the woman beside him. She was staring back at him, her chocolate-brown eyes glazed and unfocused, as if she'd survived a war.

He knew how she felt. His skin felt tight, his mind fuzzy and his groin still hurt from the intensity of his orgasm.

He was a big fan of spectacular sex. But that had been a little too spectacular. He'd never experienced anything like it before. And he wasn't altogether keen on surprises. They tended to be a lot harder to control.

She puffed out a gentle breath, an uncertain smile lifting the corner of her mouth.

'I guess you proved it,' she said.

'Proved what?'

'You do know what you're doing.'

He huffed out a laugh, the reluctant compliment breaking the tension. 'Thanks. I aim to please.'

He pushed the uneasiness to one side. What

was the big problem? Yeah, the orgasm had been intense, but it was only to be expected, given how worked up he'd been, and how beautifully she responded to him. Plus when she'd revealed what she had downstairs—that before now she'd had to instruct guys on the fine art of the female orgasm—his competitive instinct had kicked in.

Reaching across, he brushed one errant curl behind her ear. The flash of reaction as she shifted away from his touch captivated him. She really was a bunch of contradictions, both bold and cautious, experienced and yet strangely untouched.

'I should probably go home,' she said.

He smiled to himself. Did she really think he was going to let her leave that easily?

'Now why would you want to do that?' He curled his hand round her neck and felt the hammer thuds of her pulse as he stroked his thumb under her chin. 'We've only just got started.'

'Oh, come on,' she scoffed. 'You can't seriously be capable of doing it again so soon?'

'That sounds like a challenge.' He swept his hand down to her bottom. 'And I should give you fair warning, I always rise to a challenge.'

She laughed incredulously.

But as he caressed the soft, scented flesh and heard her indrawn breath even he was a little astonished by his reaction. He hadn't had powers of recovery this phenomenal since he'd been a teenager.

Go for it, Westmore, this is going to be a night to remember.

Her eyebrows shot up as she glanced down at his hardening flesh.

'We'll end up killing each other,' she remarked, the hushed tone of voice contradicted somewhat by the impish smile as she touched his erection with the tip of her finger.

'Quite possibly,' he groaned.

She gave a husky laugh as she drew her finger down the length of him.

'But I can't think of a better way to go,' he added, his rigid flesh pulsing against her palm as she began to torment him in earnest.

CHAPTER SIX

RUBY's eyelids fluttered open, then snapped shut, the blaze of sunlight searing her retinas.

She tried again, prising open one lid, then the other, and discovered a strange bedroom—which was about three times the size of the two rooms she rented in Tufnell Park.

Floor-to-ceiling French doors stood partially open, giving a panoramic view of Hampstead Heath, the dried summer grass and ancient woodland stretching up Parliament Hill into the distance. A gush of wind made her skin pebble. Then she spotted her dress draped over a leather chair, one heel lying on its side on the polished wood flooring and her lace bra hanging from the fronds of a potted Yucca plant. She groaned, her endless night of debauchery flooding back in lurid detail like an X-rated movie playing in vivid technicolor.

She hadn't just fallen off the wagon last

night, she'd flung herself head first off a cliff.

She winced, abruptly aware of the many intimate parts of her body that ached where she'd hit the ground, hard. The low murmur of deep breathing had her risking a peek over her shoulder. Lifting up on one elbow, she studied the face of the man beside her hogging most of the bed.

In the dappled sunlight, his tanned skin and the shadow of stubble on his chin gave his impossibly handsome features a dark, pagan beauty. Thick lashes touched high, hollow cheekbones, and those sensual lips— which had driven her to ecstasy too many times to count—were now partially open, the rumble of his breathing stopping just short of a snore.

She bit back another groan at the pulse of reaction in her sex.

Callum Westmore. AKA Super-stud.

No wonder the man was in a coma. They'd been at it *all* night. And not just during the night—the last time he'd forced her over that final edge before they both collapsed into an exhausted sleep, dawn had been breaking, the golden haze of sunrise gilding his skin to a burnished bronze.

Edging into a sitting position, Ruby shifted over to ease out from under the warm, heavily muscled thigh that had her legs pinned to the bed. The blue Egyptian cotton duvet slipped off his backside, and the sight of tight, beautifully sculpted buttocks sent another jolt of heat through her abused system.

She gritted her teeth. Good grief, wasn't she sore enough already?

Scooting off the bed, she gathered up her scattered clothing and tiptoed across the room in search of a bathroom, her need to pee almost as urgent as her need to get away from the object of her downfall before she did something really reckless. Like wake him up and ask for a repeat performance. Although it was difficult to imagine how much more reckless she could be after all the things she'd let him do to her last night.

The en suite bathroom was glaringly modern and expertly designed, the gleaming steel units, granite tiles, glass-brick shower cubicle and stone tub as defiantly masculine as their owner. After taking care of the toilet emergency, she searched until she found a pile of white towelling robes, all neatly folded. The fresh scent of laundry soap and fabric conditioner masked the musty scent of sex and man that clung to her skin.

Ruby hummed with pleasure as she thrust her arms into the robe. In spite of having the marauding tendencies of a Scottish Warlord, Callum Westmore clearly appreciated the creature comforts. She hissed as she belted the robe, the soft towelling like sandpaper as it touched her chest.

Opening the lapels, she gaped at the reddened skin.

Heat bloomed in her cheeks as she recalled the focused attention Cal had paid to her breasts and nipples all through the night.

Then she caught sight of herself in the mirror above the sink—and slapped a hand over her mouth to muffle the shriek.

She looked like the creature from the black lagoon.

Not only did she have whisker burn on her cheeks too, she had the worst bed hair in the history of the world ever and the smidgen of make-up she still had on was smeared under her eyes like a bruise.

Make that the creature from tart central.

Grabbing a selection of toiletries neatly arranged in a wicker basket on the sink unit, she shot over to the shower.

Damage limitation was the order of the day. She'd have to repair what she could, then get the heck out of here before her Scottish Warlord woke up and made her humiliation complete.

Mornings had never been her strong suit, and she wasn't about to risk the ignominy of the morning after with Callum. Not only did she look a fright, she hardly knew the man. And what she did know was making her very uneasy now the haze of lust had cleared.

She still didn't quite know what had got into her last night. Apart from Cal's impressive erection.

No man had ever seduced her before with such ease or efficiency. And no man had ever made her see stars. Forget stars, she'd seen a whole constellation. And then been sent soaring through the Milky Way.

While she'd been in his bed, she hadn't been able to put the whole sequence of events into any kind of perspective. But now, in the cold light of day, she could see that despite all her best-laid plans she'd barely put up a token protest last night.

But far worse than her complete lack of restraint was the way the balance of power had played out.

Right from the moment Cal had demanded that she go to dinner with him he'd been in charge. And while the end result had been mind-blowingly erotic, his ability to control her with such apparent ease bothered her. A lot.

She had a passionate, provocative nature, which was something she'd inherited from her mother. She knew that. But she'd always prided herself on never allowing it to get the better of her. The way she had bent so easily to Callum's will yesterday evening—and all through the night—felt like a betrayal of that principle, however small.

She flinched as she switched on the shower control and cool water hit her raw skin.

Now she knew she was uniquely susceptible to Callum Westmore. To the point where she could become addicted to him. It would probably be wise to steer clear of him. Once had definitely been enough.

She frowned. Fine, make that five times had definitely been enough. Or was it six?

She grabbed the shampoo and poured a large dose onto her hair as the steamy water began to soothe tired muscles. She massaged the expensive lotion into her scalp and ignored the liquid pull in her abdomen from the woodsy scent she recognised as his.

The number of times they'd done it was completely irrelevant. What mattered was that she had now alerted herself to the danger. Callum Westmore had discovered her weak spot. And if she was going to stop him from exploiting it, it would probably be wise to stop him from getting near the rest of her as well.

Ten minutes later, drenched and still a little shaky, but fortified by the plan she'd formulated, Ruby stepped out of the shower cubicle and fumbled for her robe.

'You should have woken me. I would have scrubbed your back.'

This time she didn't manage to muffle the shriek, the sound echoing against the stone tiles as she clasped the robe to her chest.

'What are you doing in here?' She shoved her arms into the garment and belted it to cover her nakedness, disturbingly aroused by the sight of him leaning nonchalantly against the units watching her.

With his long legs clad in a pair of sweat pants that hung low on narrow hips, his chest gloriously bare, his short hair sticking up in careless spikes, and a smile on his lips, he looked rumpled and buff and impossibly sexy. Resentment flared at the inevitable tug between her legs.

Without a spot of make-up on, her cheeks as shiny as beacons, the shapeless robe and her hair falling in a wet tangle down her back, she, on the other hand, probably looked about as enticing as a damp squid. Not that she wanted to entice him, mind you. It would only be counterproductive given her decision not to sleep with him again. But it was the principle of the thing. He had her at a disadvantage, and she didn't appreciate it.

'Why are you blushing?' he asked, amused. His eyes roamed over her. 'You didn't strike me as the shy type last night.'

'I'm not,' she said, although for the first time in her life she did feel a little shy. Which only annoyed her more. 'But I prefer a little privacy when I have a shower.'

'That's a shame.' He closed the distance between them in two long strides, then settled his hand on her neck. The heat sizzled straight down to her toes and made her tense. 'Because my back-scrubbing skills are legendary.'

You don't say.

She sidestepped him, grateful when the caressing palm fell away from her neck. 'I'll have to sample them another time.'

He gripped her wrist, stopping her in mid-flight. 'Stay awhile.'

She quelled the hammer of her heartbeat at the unexpected invitation, the pressure of his thumb against her pulse making it hard to stay focused.

She pulled her arm away. 'I don't think so.'

'Why not? Last night was great.'

The blunt question wasn't one she wanted to answer. Telling him she found him too overwhelming would be like waving a red rag in front of a bull. A very persistent and extremely attractive bull who already had her thighs trembling and he'd barely touched her. So she decided to go with a more straightforward excuse.

'Actually, it was too great,' she said, stifling the ridiculous blush. 'For me, anyway.'

He tilted his head to one side, the quizzical smile making him look even more assured. 'You've lost me.'

'You know.' She paused. 'It was too much... physically.'

His lips quirked and she frowned. That hadn't come out quite the way she'd planned.

He took her wrist again. 'I see.' Tugging her towards him, he wrapped an arm around her hips. She felt the prominent arousal and tried to wriggle away, shocked to feel desire welling once again.

'I don't think you do.' She braced her palms against his chest. 'I have whisker burn!'

He chuckled. 'I'm sorry, Ruby,' he murmured, not sounding all that apologetic. 'Your skin's so soft.' He touched a thumb to her cheek, the flicker of tenderness stunning her into silence. 'I have some cream that'll help. Would you like me to apply it to the affected areas?'

She shoved him back, annoyingly tempted by the offer. 'That's not a good idea. Considering.'

He laughed. 'No, probably not.'

God, she looked adorable. And so damn desirable. The flush of embarrassment and the fresh scent of his shampoo on the mass of damp curls tumbling over her shoulder tied his gut into knots. Her skin looked radiant without the carefully applied shield of make-up. Radiant and surprisingly young.

It occurred to Cal that he was even more captivated by her this morning than he had been last night. And not just by her beauty.

He'd spent ten minutes lying in bed,

listening to the shower and imagining all the things he wanted to do to her today. Most of them involving soap suds. He'd have to put those on hold.

The fact that he'd been so demanding unsettled him a little. He wasn't normally that insatiable. She'd been as enthusiastic as he had, but he still should have been a lot more careful with her. But that didn't mean they had to part company right away.

'Wait there.' Cal crossed to the cabinets and hunted up the tube of cream he'd slung in there months ago and forgotten about.

Finding it, he handed it to Ruby. 'It's supposed to be good for bruises and scraps. It should help with the whisker burn.'

Taking the tube, she read the label. 'Arnica? I wouldn't have pegged you as the new-age-remedy type.'

His lips tilted up. Why did he find her bluntness as captivating as the rest of her?

'I'm not. My sister sent me that in one of her many care packages.' Leaning back against the unit, he crossed his arms over his chest, enjoying the colour that rose in Ruby's cheeks as he studied her. Was it his imagination, or was she as captivated as he was? 'Maddy worries about me,' he added, trying to look plaintive and failing miserably, he suspected. 'And my lonely bachelor lifestyle.'

'Lonely!' She laughed. 'I'm guessing your sister doesn't know you very well.'

He smiled. 'I try to make sure of that,' he said easily.

Athough the truth was, he didn't have to try very hard. His sister was too sweet, too generous and too naive to ever understand that he preferred sex without commitment and had never once yearned for anything more.

'Well, give your sister my thanks,' Ruby said, tucking the tube into the pocket of the robe. 'On second thought, perhaps you better not.' Her eyes brightened with mischief. 'Explaining how I came to need it might be a bit awkward.' She gathered her clothes up from the counter, and nodded towards the door. 'I should be going. Thanks for last night. It was fun, despite the whisker burns.'

Forcing down the urge to chase after her, he stood motionless and relaxed as she headed towards the door. He should probably let her leave. But as she twisted the handle on the bathroom door he knew he wasn't going to.

She seemed oddly vulnerable this morning—which was something he hadn't expected. He was by nature a cynical man, the perfect storm of his childhood had seen to that. When you factored in the intellect that had allowed him to pass the bar two years early and take silk at the age of thirty-four— the youngest person at the time to be awarded the lofty position of Queen's Counsel in the history of British law—he was very rarely surprised by anything. Or anyone. Especially women.

So the unexpected always intrigued him.

And he had a rare weekend off. So why not take the opportunity to indulge his curiosity about Ruby? At least until she got her stamina back?

'Why are you in such a rush?' he remarked. 'Scared you won't be able to resist me?'

She stilled and shot round, the pink flags in her cheeks telling him he'd hit exactly the right mark.

'Your ego really is phenomenal, isn't it?' She sounded both annoyed and wary.

'So I've been told.' He levered himself up from the counter, strolled towards her, not in- sulted in the least. 'So if you're not scared, what's the big problem with us spending the day together?'

It was a dare, pure and simple. Engineered

to strike where it would get the best results—
at the independence she was so proud of.

Her eyes narrowed. 'That was sneaky.' She
gave him a light punch on the shoulder. 'How
am I supposed to say no now without looking
like a sissy?'

He laughed, pleased to see the tactic had
worked. She was going to accept the invitation. No matter how sneaky.

'So which is it? Are you a sissy or aren't
you?' he prompted.

She didn't answer, simply gave her head a
rueful shake.

He grinned. 'I'll take that as a yes, then.'

'Fine. You win.' Her bare foot tapped on
the tiles. 'But you'll have to take me home
first. I'm not going anywhere without lipstick
and some clean clothes on.'

'It's a deal,' he said, then lifted her chin
with his index finger and brushed a thumb
across her full bottom lip. 'Although if I had
my way,' he murmured, scanning her flushed
face, 'I'd be happy for you to do without
both.'

The kiss was supposed to be quick, cursory
even. But he found himself lingering, waiting
for her to soften and kiss him back. When

he eventually released her they were both breathing heavily.

She backed towards the door, gripped the door handle, the visible flutter of her pulse in the hollow of her collarbone making his gut tighten.

'And I'd be more than willing to oblige,' she shot back at him, her stance giving him a taunting glimpse of her cleavage. 'Except, you've had far too much of your own way already.'

So saying, she left the room. And shut the door behind her.

He laughed at her audacity. Then stared down.

Seemed he was going to need a cold shower before he drove her home. He whistled one of the salsa tunes from the previous evening as he dropped his sweat pants, considering where to take her for the day. It was his pick this time and he intended to make it a good one. But the whistling cut off as he dumped the sweats into the laundry basket.

When was the last time the prospect of a date had made him whistle—while sporting an erection the size of Big Ben? And when was the last time he'd been keen to spend time with a woman after they'd spent the night together, instead of itching to get her out of the door so he could have his place to himself again?

Stepping into the shower, he flipped the dial to frigid and sucked in a breath as the cold water splattered him. He set about applying logic to the situation.

Ruby only fascinated him because she wasn't like any of the other women he'd dated. That much was obvious. Spending the day together was the smart thing to do, because it would put an end to his fascination. After all, she couldn't be as clever or as exciting as she appeared—it was just her unique combination of guts, a quick wit and a great face and figure, not to mention that naughty streak, which had turned him on to the point of madness. By the time he got her back here later, they'd be able to burn off the last of the heat and their brief but enjoyable fling would be over.

The tuneless whistle began again as he reached for the soap. The glorious summer day stretched ahead of him packed full of guilty pleasures.

Which he had no reason to feel remotely guilty about.

CHAPTER SEVEN

'I LOVE this place. It's so elegant and yet so easy-going.' Ruby sighed as she took a long sip of the iced fruit juice. Slipping off her sandals, she tucked her legs under her bottom on the wide bench seat. She must have walked about five miles this morning, but instead of feeling tired she felt energised. Callum Westmore had proved to be as much fun out of the sack as he was in it.

She'd expected him to take her somewhere snooty for lunch. And had dressed down accordingly, in a casual summer dress printed with bold pink tulips—to prove she had nothing to prove. But as with the salsa club the previous evening, he'd surprised her, parking back in front of his building after the quick trip to Tufnell Park and then suggesting they walk across the Heath to the open air café that was situated in the old kitchens at Kenwood House.

The house was a restored Georgian villa used to showcase a collection of Renaissance art, but the grounds, which had also been bequeathed to the nation in 1927 and stretched across manicured lawns to the lake, were the venue for impromptu football and cricket matches, courting couples and family picnics on a hot summer afternoon.

'And so packed,' Cal said wryly, topping up her glass from the pitcher he'd ordered. 'I'm usually too busy to come here on a Saturday. I forgot how crowded this place gets at weekends.'

Propping her elbow on the table, she leaned her chin on her fist and grinned at him. 'Busy doing what exactly?' she asked, fluttering her eyelashes, unable to resist the flirtatious gesture.

The man looked ridiculously rugged and delicious in faded jeans and a polo shirt. And the morning she'd spent in his company had been so full of surprises, both small and large, she was feeling carefree and more than a tad reckless.

She'd asked herself several times as they drove to her home that morning whether she'd completely lost leave of her senses agreeing to spend the day with him.

The man was dangerous. He had an unpredictable effect on her better judgment and she needed to be a lot more careful than she had been last night. But as the day had progressed, she'd become more and more elated that he'd engineered this time together. However fleeting.

She hadn't had a weekend off in close to six months. What with the pressure of work from her business, plus the course she'd been taking in accountancy this year and the many initiatives she'd had on the go to grow A Touch of Frosting's profile in the local area, she and Ella had made a conscious decision to take the long August weekend off work as a reward. It had meant juggling orders, cooking well into the evening for two whole weeks and rearranging one of their monthly cupcake decorating classes, but they had deserved their break—even if the Cumberland interview hadn't been the icing on the cake she'd been hoping for.

Getting to spend her precious time off with an exceptionally smart, sexy and stimulating man had added to the luxury. And Ruby liked a bit of luxury in her life. Why deny it? Plus as the day had worn on she'd begun to wonder where exactly her little panic attack had come from this morning.

Okay, Cal had taken charge last night. The more she got to know him, it was pretty obvious he was a take-charge kind of guy. But she'd discovered that if she stuck to her guns she could match him—and anyway, this wasn't a war, it wasn't even a proper relationship. It was nothing more than a glorified one-night stand.

Why complicate something that simply wasn't that complicated?

The upside was, spending time with Cal out of bed hadn't been anywhere near as awkward as she would have anticipated.

As they had climbed up Parliament Hill to watch the kite enthusiasts launch their elaborate structures in the tiny breath of wind, then strolled through the ancient woodlands and shadowy copses of the Iveagh Bequest, conversation had flowed easily.

With both of them steering clear of anything too personal, they'd covered everything from the iniquities of the British Justice System to the recipe for the perfect cupcake. Callum was an articulate and enthusiastic conversationalist whose mind worked in a brilliantly logical way. Completely unlike her own—which had a tendency to drift off in all sorts of weird and wonderful directions.

Yet, despite that, he'd never once patronised her. Not even a little. And that had been the biggest surprise of all. Especially once she'd discovered exactly how brilliant he was.

After some probing, Cal had admitted that he'd sailed through school and university and then law school and the bar exams. Ruby, on the other hand, had rebelled at an early age against the strictures of the classroom.

While she was proud of what she'd achieved after leaving school at sixteen—having spent the rest of her teens attending night classes in catering college and sweating her way through three years of gruelling split shifts in her family's Italian restaurant—she'd always had a bit of a complex about her lack of academic qualifications. But while Callum clearly had a phenomenal intellect and the qualifications to prove it, he hadn't dismissed her point of view or made her feel it had less value than his own. She'd basked in the approval and appreciation in his gaze as they'd ended up in a series of lively debates.

He wasn't narrow-minded or an intellectual snob and she'd found the discovery almost as stimulating as the sight of the worn polo shirt moulding to his muscular chest or the way the short hairs on the back of his neck had begun to curl in the sluggish heat.

The other thing she'd discovered, much to her quiet astonishment, was that Callum Westmore was a hand holder. He'd clasped her fingers as soon as they'd set out across the Heath, and had hardly let go of her since.

No wonder she felt flirtatious. The rub of his palm against hers and the grip of those long, strong and exceptionally talented fingers had kept the hum of awareness sparking between them all morning.

She had no idea if he'd planned it that way. Although, from the way he made love—knowing just where to touch her to tease out the most effective response—and from the way he put forward his side of an argument—pausing to weigh each carefully constructed word or phrase of reasoning—she doubted Cal did anything without being well aware of the consequences.

Picking up the menu from the table, she fanned herself, feeling a little flushed.

She never would have guessed that she'd be so susceptible to that focused, methodical, wholly masculine approach. But one thing was for certain, the no-sex rule she'd rashly committed to that morning had become a bit of an anachronism during the course of the morning.

She had decided on a new plan as her physical awareness of him built. It was fairly simple, really. This time she would seduce him and redress the balance of power between them. Before they went their separate ways.

The only problem was, she'd been flirting with him mercilessly for over half an hour, ever since they'd sat down to eat a delicious meal of rosemary potatoes and roast guinea fowl, and he had yet to take the bait.

'Is that a personal or a professional question?' The rough tone of his voice made her heartbeat scramble. Did she finally have a nibble?

'Why don't you take a wild guess?'

Reaching across the table, he lifted her hand, threaded his fingers through hers. 'Is this your veiled way of indicating you've recovered from the whisker burn?'

Turning her hand to clasp his, she brought his fingers to her lips, and licked along his knuckles. She felt him shudder and grinned. 'I wouldn't call it veiled, Callum.'

He choked out a laugh, his fingers fisting

in hers as he stood up and pulled her off the bench. 'You are a very naughty girl, Ruby.' One large hand settled on her hip as he drew her easily against him. 'I hope you realise you're playing with fire.'

Ruby's heartbeat sped up. Settling her free hand on his nape, she caressed the short hairs that had fascinated her all day. 'I adore playing with fire.'

She ran her thumb across his cheek, marvelling at the renewed rasp of stubble even though he had shaved only a few hours before. 'It's so exhilarating to tame.'

'Tame?' His brows lifted and the smile in his eyes dimmed. 'I'm not in the market to be tamed, Ruby. You do realise that.'

The warning was clear and unequivocal. Embarrassment stained Ruby's cheeks at the silly little stab of hurt.

'Well, that's good, Cal, because neither am I,' she said, determined to believe it. She'd never be foolish enough to misconstrue her pleasure in the day they'd spent together as a desire for something more. 'I thought you knew,' she added. 'I'm simply using you for sex.'

However much fun they'd had, Cal was the very last man she'd want to get into a relationship with. He was far too… Far too everything. Too smart, too charming, too controlled. He didn't have a single chink in his armour. Which made him perfect fling material. But not the sort of man any sensible woman would want to risk falling for.

He grinned and the look of caution disappeared. 'Using *me*?' He twisted his head to nip her thumb. 'I'd like to see you try,' he replied, the uncomfortable moment gone.

Ruby smiled back, refusing to let the little jolt ruin a perfectly good seduction. 'That sounds like a challenge,' she murmured, letting the heady thrill of arousal course through her.

Gripping his shoulders, she raised up on tiptoes to reach his lips.

'And I should give you fair warning, I always rise to a challenge.' She threw his words back at him, flicking her tongue across his mouth then drawing back. He groaned, cool palms spanning her waist then running up her sides as he dragged her close and sank into the kiss.

His breath gushed out as he pulled away. 'I suggest we take this indoors, before you get us both arrested.'

She giggled. 'Spoilsport…' She bent to pick

up her sandals, laughing as he pressed his palm to the small of her back to direct her towards the exit. She noticed the envious stares from a group of young women sitting at the entrance of the packed café—and had a momentary fantasy in which she was Cleopatra, and Callum her Mark Antony.

Was there anything more exhilarating, she wondered, than bringing a strong man to his knees? This weekend was about letting her inner flirt off the leash for a short while and reconnecting with the empowering pleasures of great sex. And nothing more.

The fact that Callum was on exactly the same wavelength had to be a good thing.

CHAPTER EIGHT

THE raucous ringing of the phone interrupted the long languid sigh as Ruby stretched, every cell in her body tingling with afterglow.

'Ignore it.' Cal's hand caressed her bottom. 'The machine will pick up in a minute.'

Easing into a sitting position, Ruby leaned over him and grinned. With his eyes closed, his short hair furrowed into tufts and his cheeks flushed beneath his tan, he looked satisfied and ever so slightly shattered.

Cleopatra, eat your heart out.

Ruby Delisantro had brought her Scottish Warlord to his knees. And not just metaphorically speaking. They'd grabbed a cab back to his flat, not wanting to waste time walking back across the Heath, and then jumped each other. But instead of letting him dictate all the moves, she'd managed to surprise even herself with her desire to taste and touch him in ways that would make him beg.

And okay, maybe he hadn't exactly begged, but he'd come pretty damn close.

'What's the matter, Westmore?' she asked sweetly, brushing the damp hair back from his brow. 'Too exhausted to even answer your own phone?'

He opened his eyes, a slow smile forming, the phone still blaring from the living room, then grabbed her round the waist and rolled over, pinning her beneath him. 'I wouldn't get too cocky if I were you, Delisantro.'

She laughed, loving the way his eyes lit with challenge.

'Why not? I made you beg.'

A bit of an exaggeration, but she intended to push her advantage, as far as was humanly possible. She'd proved that their connection was just about great sex and all was right with her world again.

'You're good,' he said, the appreciative chuckle pleasing her immensely. 'But you're not that good.' Framing her face, he pressed his lips below her ear, began to nuzzle the sensitive skin. 'Give me a couple of minutes and I'll prove it.'

'A couple of minutes!' She sniggered, her

body so enervated it was almost a sin. 'Give me a break, you're going to need more time than that.'

'Don't be too sure.'

Knowing him, he probably wasn't joking, but she scoffed anyway. Because it was required.

His disembodied voice, measured and businesslike, echoed from the living room, asking the unknown caller to leave a message.

'At last,' he said, then started nuzzling again. 'Now where were we?'

Ruby shivered, ready to let him do all the work this time, when a worried female voice sliced through the erotic fog.

'Cal, where are you? You said you'd come down for Mia's birthday party this weekend. I expected you over an hour ago. Are you all right? Has something happened?'

The voice continued in the same vein as Cal swore and raised his head. 'Hold that thought,' he said. 'I won't be long.'

Levering off the bed, he grabbed his jeans, tugged them on and left the room.

Ruby lurched up, the playful mood destroyed. The woman sounded upset. But more than that she'd seen the sudden flicker of guilt cross Cal's face before he'd masked it.

Slipping out of bed, Ruby grabbed the towelling robe off the floor and followed Cal down the corridor. Her throat closed at the thought that the caller might be his girlfriend. Why hadn't she asked if he was seeing someone? And who the hell was Mia? She rubbed her arms as the cold weight of disillusionment coiled in her belly.

Stopping in the doorway of a large, expensively furnished and scrupulously tidy living room, Ruby watched Cal pick up the phone. He had his back to her, his shoulders stiffening as he spoke into the receiver.

'Maddy, calm down. I'm here,' he said, his voice sharp with impatience. He ran his fingers through his hair as he listened to the reply.

Maddy. The sister Cal had mentioned that morning. But even as Ruby made the connection the rush of relief she would have expected refused to come.

'I forgot about the party,' he continued, sounding annoyed now. 'It's not the end of the world. Mia's three, she won't even notice if I'm there or not.'

Ruby stepped back. She should return to the bedroom before he caught her eavesdropping, but the sound of Cal's voice—so stiff and irritable—made her stop in the doorway.

The long-forgotten memory of pain and humiliation rose back to the surface as she continued to listen to him reason coldly with his sister.

'It's too late now,' Cal argued, his voice devoid of emotion.

He sounded like a stranger, the flat, dismissive tone nothing like the relaxed, charismatic man she had thought she knew. How could she have been so wrong about him?

'I'm up to my eyes in work,' he added, the brittle excuse nothing short of brutal. 'I can't make it this weekend.'

Ruby straightened, pushing away from the doorframe. That was a lie. Why was he lying? Then she knew and a tidal wave of guilt assailed her. He hadn't been busy with work. He'd been busy with her.

She walked silently back to the bedroom, tuning out the conversation she'd overheard—and wished she hadn't—hideously disappointed not just with Callum now, but also with herself.

She hadn't just been wrong about him, she'd also been wrong about the situation she'd happily flung herself into.

Sex always came with complications. Even the wild weekend fling kind.

'Look, Maddy, I'll think about it. Okay?'

'Please come, Cal. It's been months since we've seen you,' Maddy said with a weary lack of expectation. 'We'll hold dinner for you.'

'I'll call you back and let you know.' Cal slapped the phone back into its cradle and rubbed his hand across the nape of his neck where the muscles had tightened like a vice. He wanted to punch his fist through a wall. How did she always do this to him? Make him give in when they both knew it would do no good.

Perching on the edge of the sofa, he crossed his legs at the ankles, sank his chin onto his chest and buried his hands in his pockets. It wasn't an emotion he was particularly proud of, but he let the mix of frustration and regret that conversations with his sister always caused wash over him. And then cursed softly.

He and Maddy were different people. They wanted different things out of life and she'd never been able to understand that. So why the hell should he feel guilty about avoiding seeing her and her family? Visiting his sister, seeing the way she and her husband Rye looked at each other, made him uncomfortable and the adoration of their daughter Mia—which made no sense to him at all—only made the discomfort more intense.

He lifted his head and stared at the ceiling, let out a heavy sigh.

Stop sulking, Westmore. You've only yourself to blame for this mess.

He'd been monumentally stupid. Stupid to forget Mia's birthday party. And even more stupid to forget to phone Maddy with a decent excuse well in advance.

The thought of Ruby lying in his bed, her beautiful body all soft and scented and flushed with afterglow, had some of the guilt and tension easing out of his shoulders—but none of the frustration.

He didn't like visiting Maddy at the best of times. But, damn it, he had other plans now.

If he'd paid more attention he could have spent the rest of the weekend availing himself of Ruby Delisantro's considerable charms. But now he was forced to make a choice between doing what he wanted or doing what he felt obliged to do—which would mean a six-hour drive down to Cornwall and then spending the rest of his weekend off getting bombarded with relationship advice he didn't want from his sister.

He pushed off the couch, pulled his hands out of his pockets and rubbed his palms down his face.

'Damn it!'

He loved his sister, and, however suspicious he might be of the new, improved and blissfully happy Maddy—and however much he might hate getting pushed into doing something he didn't want to do—he'd heard the plea in her voice.

He made his way down the corridor. Realising there was another problem.

If he left for Cornwall, what did he do about Ruby?

He caught her scent as he passed the open bathroom door and the memory of her full lips on his erect flesh brought a pulse of heat so intense, the problem came into sharp vivid focus. He still wanted her. And not just in bed. She'd captivated him today while they were on the Heath. She was bright, beautiful and remarkably forthright, her mental agility challenging him every step of the way. And best of all, she'd been quick to agree with him that she wasn't looking for anything more than great sex and good company.

She still wasn't his type. She was far too unpredictable for that. And as much fun as they'd had together he doubted she'd settle for being his playmate for long. Sooner or later she would have expectations. But that didn't alter the fact that he didn't want to let her walk. Not while she was still willing to play.

He glanced at the clock on the wall. Two o'clock. If he decided to go, he had an hour before he would have to leave. Question was, did that give him enough time to finesse Ruby into agreeing to another wild night when he got back? A slow grin lifted his lips. With her naked and in his bed, and given his superior powers of persuasion, the odds had to be in his favour.

Thrusting open the bedroom door, he came to an abrupt halt, the grin flat-lining. What was she doing out of bed, with her clothes mostly on, her hair damp and her shoulders twisted as if she were trying to contort herself into a pretzel?

Seeing him, she huffed and dropped her arms, then gathered the wet strands of hair into a bunch, flicked them over her shoulder.

'Could you zip me up? I'd have to dislocate a shoulder to do it myself.'

'You're dressed,' he said, dully. 'And you've had a shower.' He knew he was stating the obvious, but… What the hell was going on?

'I've got to shoot off.' Her voice was frigid, the sultry, sexy warmth of ten minutes before gone.

'Since when?' he asked, not liking the feeling of confusion—or the way his heart had kicked up a beat.

She bent to wiggle her toes into her shoes. 'Since now.' She dipped her head to her shoulder. 'So could you please do the honours?'

He stayed where he was. He could hear irritation and frustration, but there was something else beneath it. He didn't like that either.

'Is there a problem here?' he asked. 'Because if there is I'd like to know what it is.'

'The problem is I'm leaving and I can't do it with my dress half off. So do you mind?'

He crossed to her, pulled her round to face him. 'Yeah, actually I do. You're pissed off. And I'd like to know why.'

Was she annoyed that he'd left her to go answer the call to his sister? The reaction seemed petty and childish and nothing like the woman he'd spent the day with. But then, how well did he really know her?

'I'd like to leave, please.' That wasn't just impatience he could see in her eyes, it was accusation.

'Why? You were pretty damn keen to stay a few minutes ago. What's changed?'

'You have.' Her eyes narrowed and he saw temper and disappointment. 'You're not the man I thought you were.'

'I beg your pardon?'

'You heard me.' She marched past him, obviously giving up on her dress.

He took her arm, hauled her back. 'Humour me. I want an explanation.' No way was he letting her walk off without one.

'Fine.' She jerked her arm out of his, pushed her chin up. 'I don't like the way you talked to your sister. It was unnecessarily cruel. I've been there. I know what it's like to be rejected like that by someone you love. And believe me, it's not pleasant. So in the interests of sisterly solidarity, I'm leaving.'

'Sisterly…?' He was so stunned at the outburst, he had to grab her again before she got out of the door. 'Hang on a damn minute.'

'Let go of my arm.'

'For one,' he said, tightening his grip, 'she's

not your sister. In fact, you don't even know Maddy. So why the hell do you even care how I talk to her?' He could have added it was none of her business and she shouldn't have been eavesdropping in the first place, but he decided to let that pass. Seeing the mutinous expression on her face, he was more interested in knowing where the hell this was all coming from.

'I could hear how upset she was on the phone.' She tried to shrug him off; he held firm. 'You brushed her off. I thought better of you than that. But I can see I was wrong. Clearly it was more convenient for you to spend the weekend seducing some woman you've only just met than keeping a promise you made to your sister. That's not something I want to be a party to.'

He wanted to shout at her, frustration warring with temper, but beneath the accusation and self-righteous indignation in her voice he could hear the distress. So he resisted the urge to roar.

'You know, if you're going to eavesdrop on private conversations you should at least do it properly and listen to the whole thing.'

'I heard enough. I heard you tell her you couldn't come. That you were too busy with work. When we both know work had nothing to do with—'

'I prefer not to talk to my sister about my sex life. If that's okay with you,' he interrupted, letting sarcasm drip. 'And I didn't forget to go deliberately. I got a little sidetracked by a certain woman who has been happily seducing me right back.'

'Even so, you're not going, when you should—'

'I *am* going,' he interrupted, the sharp words stopping her in mid-rant. 'In fact, I'm leaving as soon as I can get packed.' Or he was now. 'Even though it's going to be a pain in the backside. Maddy and her family live in Cornwall, for God's sake. It's a six-hour drive and you and I both know I didn't exactly get a whole lot of sleep last night.'

'You're going? Really?'

'Yes, I am.' Quite why he'd made up his mind on the spur of the moment, he didn't know. But he was stuck with the decision now. 'My sister may drive me nuts most of the time, but I wouldn't deliberately set out to disappoint her or my niece.'

Her arm went limp in his grasp, the colour riding her cheeks like a beacon as the tension drained out of her. 'I didn't... I thought you were…' Her voice trailed off, the guilty flush heating.

'See what I mean about the eavesdropping?' he said.

She dipped her head. When her gaze lifted back to his, he saw contrite and embarrassed. Not a look he would ever have associated with her. But then she'd never been predictable.

He always made a point of not delving too deeply into a woman's motivations, because that way lay madness. But the itch of discomfort wasn't doing a damn thing to halt his curiosity. Why had she flown off the handle like that? She'd mentioned being rejected by someone she loved. And he suddenly wanted to know who. And why.

'I shouldn't have butted in. Or jumped to conclusions,' she added. 'I'm really sorry.'

'You know, you owe me,' he said, the solution to his problem popping into his head with startling clarity. 'You made assumptions about me that weren't true—and you should make it up to me.'

She'd forced his hand, made him agree to visit Maddy when he hadn't properly weighed up the options. He deserved some payback for that.

'How?' she asked blankly.

Cal silenced the little voice in his head telling him to stop and think this through. So what if he was using whatever it was that had caused that passionate reaction against her? And so what if the urge to keep her with him was unprecedented? This solution would make the trip to Maddy's a lot more bearable, and give them both the chance to finish this thing once and for all.

'I want you to come with me.'

CHAPTER NINE

RUBY gave a half-laugh, sure he had to be joking, but Cal didn't laugh back. In fact, he didn't even smile. 'You're not serious? I don't know your sister,' she spluttered.

'That didn't bother you a moment ago.'

He couldn't possibly be serious. The idea was preposterous. But even more preposterous was the fanciful little bump in her heartbeat at the determination in his voice.

'You'll like Maddy,' he said, as if that were even relevant.

'But this is a family affair, and I'm a stranger. Why would you even want me there?' she said. She'd made a foolish mistake, not just jumping to conclusions, but getting worked up about what she'd overheard in the first place. How he behaved towards his sister—or anyone else—shouldn't have mattered to her in the slightest.

His gaze roamed over her, making heat curl and twist in her abdomen. 'You mean apart from all the obvious reasons.'

'Yes, apart from those.' She crossed her arms over her chest, refusing to let him side-track her—even if her hormones were dancing a jig again at the sight of his naked chest. 'Sex isn't a good enough reason to introduce a woman you barely know to your family.'

'I think we've got to know each other pretty well, actually,' he said.

She shivered as his thumb stroked across her collarbone.

He laughed, the sound rough with arousal. 'See what I mean?'

She batted his hand away, colour rising to her cheeks at the quiver at her core, the quick-fire response making her feel oddly vulnerable. 'You're going to have to do better than that. It's not like we can spend the whole time we're there in bed. I'll have to talk to your sister.' She threw up her hands. 'How are you going to introduce me? I'm not even a proper girlfriend.' How could she have forgotten that a moment ago?

Placing a hand on her hip, he tugged her easily towards him. 'I'll tell her you're a friend. She'll be so excited to see you she won't delve too deeply.'

Ruby's brow creased. 'Why would she be excited to see me?'

He dipped his head, touched her forehead to his before giving a hefty sigh. 'All right, I'll come clean. Ever since Maddy's got married, had a child, she's made it her mission in life to find me that special someone. So I can be as blissfully happy as she is.'

Beneath the amusement, Ruby heard the sharp edge of cynicism. 'And you don't like that?'

'I hate it. I'm not the love and marriage type,' he said, making it sound like an affliction. 'But she won't take the hint. Maddy's a fixer. She always has been, ever since we were kids. If she sees a problem, she tries to fix it. Even if the problem doesn't exist.'

'Maybe she just wants you to be happy,' Ruby said, finding it sad he didn't appreciate having someone who cared that much about him.

He shot her a rueful look. 'You are such a girl.'

'How observant.'

He smiled. 'The point is I am happy. Or I would be if I could visit my sister without getting the third degree about my love life.' He touched her cheek. 'But now I'm thinking, with you there…as a very sexy distraction… things could be a whole lot easier.'

Ruby forced out a laugh, determined to be amused instead of insulted—or hurt—by the suggestion. This was good. He had a logical reason for wanting her along. She should be logical back. 'So I'd be, like, your stunt girlfriend?'

He nodded, not looking remotely ashamed at the ploy to fool his sister.

'That is *so* like a guy. Why can't you just be honest with her? Tell her you're not ready for that sort of commitment.'

'Believe me, I've told her I'll *never* be ready for that sort of commitment. But Maddy won't buy it. She's convinced herself her marriage is perfect, and it'll always be that way, despite all the evidence to the contrary.'

Again she heard the note of cynicism, sharpened by bitterness—and wondered what had made Cal so sure his sister's marriage was doomed to failure.

'Plus you have no idea how persistent Maddy is,' he added. 'So you have to come with me. And protect me from her.'

'So now who's the sissy?' she teased, pretty

sure Callum Westmore had never needed any-one's protection.

But she could feel her resolve weakening.

The man had charm to spare and he knew how to use it. But more than that, she was oddly flattered by his persistence. And desperately curious. Seeing someone in their home environment was always revealing. And there were so many things about Cal that she wanted to know.

'And Cornwall's incredible at this time of year.' His lips lifted in an assured smile and her pulse slowed.

She laughed at the temptation in his eyes. 'Oh, all right, then, Counsellor. I'll come,' she said, determined to ignore the panicked flutter of her pulse. They were fine, they were back to where they were supposed to be. Shallow and sexy, right where they'd been before she'd overreacted and made a twit of herself over the phone call.

'Great.'

Warmth spread through her system at the approval turning his irises to a rich emerald.

'But only if we stop by my flat so I can pack an overnight bag,' she finished, not wanting to be a complete pushover.

'You're on.'

He tugged her close, his lips covering hers in a lazy kiss. She opened her mouth, making the warmth shoot to blazing heat—and burn off all her lingering doubts.

As they sped down the motorway in Cal's flashy Italian convertible, with the roof up and two hastily packed overnight bags stowed in the back seat, Ruby stared at the not altogether sumptuous scenery of the M4 corridor and tried not to let the doubts resurface.

Callum Westmore was dangerous. But she could handle him and this 'thing' between them just fine, because it was nothing more than a straightforward mix of heat and curiosity.

She'd never be foolish enough to get serious about someone as dominant as Cal, because she liked to be the one in charge too much. But that didn't mean she couldn't satisfy the heat. And the curiosity.

Leaning forward, she turned down the soulful ballad blaring out of the car speakers from the golden oldies radio station he'd chosen.

'What did you mean,' she asked, shifting in her seat to look at Cal, 'when you said "despite evidence to the contrary"?'

'Sorry?' He sent her a cursory glance as he flipped up his indicator to swing into the fast lane.

'You said something about your sister, believing her marriage was perfect, despite evidence to the contrary. What did that mean? Do you know something she doesn't? Is her husband cheating on her?' The thought depressed her. She wouldn't wish that kind of heartache on any woman—or man, for that matter.

'Not as far as I know,' he said. 'Rye seems like a nice enough guy.' The observation sounded strangely detached.

'So what did you mean by evidence to the contrary? What evidence?'

'I guess I meant marriage generally.' He shrugged, shifting down a gear to overtake a lorry. 'Our parents' marriage was a disaster and they made sure we knew it. That was hard on Maddy.'

'What about you?'

'Hmm?' he said, distracted as he checked his blind spot.

'What about you? Wasn't it hard for you too?' Had she finally found a chink in his armour?

'Me?' He gave a hollow laugh as if the

suggestion was ridiculous. 'Not particularly.' He sent her an easy smile. 'Maddy's a romantic. She wanted their marriage to work. I didn't care.'

Ruby frowned. What a strange thing to say. Surely you didn't have to be a romantic to want your parents' marriage to work?

She wouldn't call herself a romantic because she'd seen how the romantic ideal had failed to save her own family. But that hadn't made her lose sight of all the good things marriage had to offer.

From the conversation they'd shared that morning on the Heath, it was clear Cal prided himself on being pragmatic and logical. But had a difficult childhood turned that pragmatism and logic to cynicism?

'When people fall in love, marriage is the logical next step,' she remarked. 'That's not always a bad thing, surely?'

Cal groaned inwardly as he eased his foot off the accelerator and cruised into the inside lane. The L word. How did women always find a way to insinuate it into any conversation about relationships? And why had he thought Ruby would be different? 'I've got to tell you,' he said. 'I didn't have you pegged as the hopeless romantic type.'

'I'm not.' She snorted out an incredulous laugh. 'Marriage is complicated. Believe me I know that. My parents had what everyone thought was a good marriage on the surface. Solid, sweet, loving, supportive. But when it ended, it turned out there was a lot going on beneath the surface.'

'So they got divorced. That's a good thing,' Cal remarked forcefully.

Normally, he avoided personal conversations with women he was sleeping with—but the sudden sadness in her voice had tugged at his usual reserve.

'You were better off,' he added. 'I wish to hell my parents had had the guts to get a divorce.'

'My parents didn't get divorced,' she said. 'Their marriage ended when my mother died.'

Cal's fingers tightened on the wheel at Ruby's toneless words, completely devoid of self-pity. Now would probably be a good time to change the subject. But instead of the impersonal apology that was supposed to come out of his mouth, he heard himself saying: 'How old were you when she died?'

'Ten.'

Damn. His chest tightened at the curt reply.

'That must have been really tough,' he murmured, surprised by the surge of sympathy. His own mother had never had much time for him or Maddy. She'd always been far too busy navigating the wreck of her marriage. But losing her would have left a hole. If only a small one. Thinking of Ruby suffering such a loss at such a young age made him want to offer comfort. Not something he had a lot of experience with.

She gave her head a slight shake. 'It was, but she'd been sick for over a year. What was much tougher was discovering right after she'd died that she wasn't the perfect person I'd always thought she was. Far from it, actually.'

He concentrated on the road ahead, debating whether to ask the obvious next question. It wasn't his business, but the bitter disillusionment in her tone was something he understood only too well.

'What did you discover?' he asked.

Seemed his fascination with Ruby hadn't dimmed in the least, and his usual caution had deserted him.

CHAPTER TEN

RUBY frowned, not sure how she'd ended up talking about her mother to Cal of all people. It wasn't as if what her mother had done was a big secret or anything. But she didn't normally discuss this stuff, particularly with men she was dating. It was a total downer.

'Cal, it's okay, you don't have to listen to my life story,' she said, trying to deflect him.

'I know that.'

'You can't be remotely interested.'

'I wouldn't have asked if I wasn't,' he said, not sounding deterred in the least. 'Come on. Whatever she did, it can't have been all that terrible.'

'You think?' Animosity scoured her throat. 'How about she screwed another man just after she married my dad. Got pregnant. And then passed the baby off as his?'

The words spewed out, harsh and judgmental.

'Okay, that's pretty bad,' Cal said beside her, the measured response making her suddenly feel ashamed. Not just for her anger, but for the bitterness behind it.

'Actually, it wasn't that bad.' She huffed out a breath, studying Cal's profile. 'It was only one night, and Mum was barely nineteen. The guy in question was rich, handsome, sophisticated, by all accounts a total sex machine and he seduced her.'

Cal's strong hand gripped the gear shift and she felt the pulse of heat at the memory of his fingers on her skin. Perhaps it was about time she forgave her mother. After last night, she had firsthand experience of just how irresistible spectacular sex could be.

'You're more forgiving than I would be,' Cal said. Almost as if he had read her thoughts. 'So your father was the one who rejected you, then? When he found out you were illegitimate?'

'Sorry?'

'You said you knew what it was like to be rejected by someone you love. When you got upset with me about Maddy.'

Colour hit her cheeks at the reminder. God,

had she actually said that out loud? She really had lost the plot earlier.

'The baby in question wasn't me. It was my brother, Nick.'

'I see,' he said carefully, then glanced towards her, his emerald eyes narrowed. 'So who was it, then? Who rejected you?'

He sounded annoyed, which didn't make any sense.

'I suppose I was referring to my brother, Nick. It has to do with what happened on the night my mum died.' She paused, not sure how to explain it all. 'When my dad found out he wasn't Nick's biological father.' She stopped abruptly. Why was she talking about this? It was way too personal. 'It's a long story. And really boring actually,' she finished.

'Don't forget we've still got five hours on the road. I can't think of another way to pass the time.' A smile tilted his lips. 'That's legal while I'm driving, that is.'

She smiled back, the teasing comment easing some of the tension.

'It's not just long, remember. It's boring,' she replied. 'I wouldn't want you lapsing into a coma while you have my life in your hands.'

He laughed, then put his hand on her knee,

squeezed. 'If you see me starting to nod off at the wheel, poke me in the ribs.'

The light words and gesture were so tender and so surprising she felt an odd constriction in her throat. She looked away, the weight of his palm having a strange effect on her.

She'd never talked about this before, but she couldn't quite deny the urge to talk about it now. Maybe it was just that Cal's logical, analytical, unemotional approach was seductive. Was it possible that he could shed some light on all the conflicting emotions from that long ago summer?

How often had she asked herself if she could have done more? Maybe if she'd been older, or more aware of what was going on sooner, she could have solved the problem before it had become so huge it had been insurmountable.

'All right, but, just so you know, you can stop me any time if this gets tedious.' She took a deep breath.

'Start from the beginning.' His hand stroked her thigh. 'The night your mum died.'

'Okay.' She let go of the breath. This shouldn't be that hard. Not after all this time. 'It was sweltering that night. My dad had closed the restaurant the day before. Which felt so weird.'

'Your dad owns a restaurant?'

'He used to, a little Tuscan place not far from the house I live in now. Nothing fancy, but my parents had put their whole lives into the business after they arrived from Italy. They ran it together with two other staff. Nick and me helped out in the mornings before school and on weekends.'

'When you were ten?' He sounded astonished.

She grinned, recalling how much she had adored the constant bustle of the kitchen—watching her mum and dad work side by side. It had always made her feel so secure. Funny to think that image could still make her feel good. Even though she knew now the sense of security had been false.

'Yes, well, I pretended to help and Nick did most of the work, bussing tables and doing the dirtiest kitchen duty. I loved it. He didn't. Even before…' Her voice trailed off. Did she really want to relive any of this?

'So that explains your cupcake capabilities,' Cal remarked.

'Yes,' she said, the interruption successfully

shifting her focus back to the task at hand. 'I come from a long line of food aficionados.'

'But Nick wasn't into it?'

'Nick hated everything about the catering industry. The noise, the constant stress and activity,' she murmured. 'But it wasn't just that. There was something wrong between Nick and Mum. Even then.' Why had she always refused to admit that until now?

'How do you mean?'

'She was so flamboyant. So passionate about everything. She had this huge appetite for life that spilled over into everything she did. But with Nick it was different.' Ruby tried to push the guilt to one side, but it refused to budge. 'She never hugged him or kissed him with anything like the same enthusiasm she did me. I guess my dad noticed too, because he filled the gap. He was brilliant with Nick, bringing him out of his shell, praising everything he did. But the night she died, that all changed.' She rubbed the heel of her hand on her breastbone. The sick, choked up feeling came back.

'We were all hurting,' she whispered above the quiet hum of the car. 'She was such a big part of our lives, our family and now she was gone. And as hard as it had been to watch the way she suffered with the cancer, the finality was worse. Nick said something. I can't even remember what. And our dad, it was like he turned on him. He started ranting in Italian. Something about not wanting to look at Nick, not wanting to hear him speak.' Tears scorched her throat, making it difficult to speak. 'Nick went white with shock. I started crying. I begged Dad to stop. I know I grabbed hold of him and clung on. And he did stop. He apologised. And then he started to weep. He held me so tight I found bruises on my arms the next day. But he wouldn't hug Nick. He wouldn't even look at him.'

She pushed away the tear that had slipped out with her fist. Her breath hitching. God, when was she finally going to get over this?

'When did you find out about Nick being illegitimate?'

She swallowed. Cal's astute question bringing back the agony she'd gone through at the time. 'I overheard my dad and Nick talking on the day of her funeral.' She sighed. 'Mum told Dad the truth on the night she died.' Ruby paused, the sense of betrayal, of confusion still stupidly fresh. Not just because of the infidelity, but because her mother had confessed. Why had she confessed and destroyed everything? 'My dad told Nick it didn't matter. That he didn't care. That he'd forgiven my mother and that he still considered him to be his son. But Nick couldn't forgive her. He retreated into this sullen, angry silence. I tried to reach him.' She sighed. 'I had this mad idea that if I loved him more, I could make it up to him.'

'Not mad,' Cal interrupted, with implacable certainty. 'Understandable. My sister did the same thing whenever my parents had one of their break-ups. She always tried to fix it. I think she thought if she could be a better daughter that somehow things would be all right.'

'That's it. That's exactly it,' she said, pathetically pleased to finally have those immature yearnings validated. 'I thought the same thing. Our family was falling apart before my eyes. And there was no way to solve it. To make it better.'

'What happened to Nick?'

'He became a different person. He used to be so sensitive. So open. But after Mum died, he started to stay out late, hang out with the worst kids in the neighbourhood, bunked off school, got into fights. He wouldn't talk to me. And him and Dad argued all the time—I suppose he was trying to test if my dad really loved him or not. And then when he was sixteen, they had this massive row one night and he left. My dad tried to find him. But he was just gone.'

'So you never saw your brother again?'

If only it could have been that simple.

'I contacted him three years ago when my dad had a massive heart attack. Dad had to stop working and we sold the restaurant. I knew he was dying. He knew it too. And he asked me to find Nick. He wanted to see him one more time. So I hired an agency.' To think even then, she'd still held out some hope that she could fix things. 'Turns out he lives in San Francisco. He's a scriptwriter. In Hollywood,' she added, pride thickening her voice despite everything. 'It took me three weeks of phone calls to his agent and then his PA before he called me back.' She shook her head, the agony and devastation still far too real. 'He didn't want to know.' She blinked, the sheen of tears turning the motorway's grass verges to a misty green. 'I rang him twice more, when Dad started to deteriorate, and he took the calls, but I couldn't make him budge.'

'What did he say?'

'That he didn't want to see Dad again.' She gulped down the silly sting of pain. 'That was the worst bit, he kept referring to him as "your dad" like they weren't even related. I lost my temper with him. I shouted, I pleaded, I argued and begged. But he wouldn't listen. Dad died a few weeks later. I sent Nick an invite to the funeral and he didn't show.' She turned to Cal, saw the sharp frown of concentration on his brow. 'So there you have it. The long and boringly anecdotal reason why I made such an idiot of myself this afternoon when your sister rang. I heard you talking to her and it was like all those feelings came back—of pain and frustration and helplessness—and I transferred all my unhappiness with Nick onto you.'

Looking at the rigid line of Cal's jaw, the muscle twitching as he kept his eyes on the road ahead, she wondered again at the idiotic impulse, but still felt relieved that she finally had a decent explanation. Her volatile reaction had never had anything to do with her and Cal. It had always been about her and Nick.

'I expect you're probably questioning the state of my mental health at the moment.' She gave a strained laugh. 'And I wouldn't blame you in the least. But, honestly, I don't usually make such a complete twit of myself. Especially not on such short acquaintance.'

'There's no need to apologise again,' he murmured. 'Given the context, your reaction makes sense.' His eyes drifted over her face and figure before returning to the road ahead. 'You're a passionate person.' His lips turned up at the corner. 'I've got several reasons to be grateful for that.'

Turning towards the console, Ruby drew her knees up, settled her cheek against the deep bucket seat and gazed at the man beside her. 'You know, you're an exceptionally good listener,' she murmured, knowing he'd been much more than that. With his straightforward questions and observations he'd helped her see the breakdown of her family in a new light. She could see now she'd tried, she'd done her best and she had to stop blaming herself for something that had never been in her power to fix.

His brow lifted. 'It's part of my job to listen,' he said, but she detected a note of caution that made her smile. He sounded taken aback, wary and even a little embarrassed. Who would have suspected that her Scottish Warlord would be flummoxed by a simple compliment?

Her eyelids grew heavy as she breathed in the pleasant scent of new leather that permeated the car. She stretched as a huge yawn overtook her. The outpouring of emotion had drained her.

'I've hit the wall.' She yawned again, all the activity of the last twenty-four hours catching up with her in one energy-sapping rush.

'Tilt the seat back and get some sleep,' he said, switching the radio back up and adjusting the station until an old reggae song crooned gently out of the speakers. 'We've got hours yet.'

Fatigue tugged at Ruby's limbs making them feel weightless as the quiet hum of the powerful engine lulled her into sleep. Her lips tipped up as she floated on a wave of exhaustion. Incredible to think she'd laid eyes on Callum Westmore for the first time only yesterday morning. The man certainly knew how to make an impression on a girl. In more ways than one.

Cal's knuckles whitened on the steering wheel as he flashed the car ahead of them in the outside lane, which was poking along at a sedate ten miles under the speed limit. The surge of adrenaline that coursed through him as he pressed his foot on the accelerator and flew past it made the anger in his gut harden.

Right about now he'd like to take a horsewhip to Nick Delisantro.

Ruby's big brother sounded like a self-serving, self-absorbed son of a bitch. Maybe Cal was never going to be a candidate for the Brother of the Year Award, but he'd never treat Maddy with the cold, careless contempt this Nick guy had treated Ruby.

Hearing the hitch in Ruby's voice as she'd talked about the phone calls, he knew what it must have cost her—his proud and passionate Ruby—to watch her father die knowing she hadn't been able to fulfil his dying wish. Nick Delisantro's selfishness beggared belief, the guy needed to be...

Whoa there. 'What the...?' The whispered curse burst out.

His Ruby. Where the hell had that come from?

He slanted a sideways look at the woman curled up in the passenger seat, her wildly curling hair framing high cheekbones, the dusky skin a pale gold in the sunlight. Drawing a deep breath into his lungs—he let it out gradually. Relaxing his death grip on the steering wheel, he glanced at the speedometer and slowed the car.

Ruby Delisantro was not 'his Ruby'. Not even close. He hardly knew her.

All right, maybe he'd had some of the best sex of his life in her company.

Heat swelled in his groin as he thought back to what she'd done to him that afternoon.

Make that *the* best sex of his life. And he planned to have more before the weekend was over. But come tomorrow evening, when they got back to London, their fling would be over.

She was not his. And she never would be.

He tapped his thumb on the steering wheel. Spotting the sign for the M5, he merged into the inside lane to take the exit signposting The South West.

He didn't do long-term relationships. He didn't like getting that involved in other people's lives, because he hated the lack of privacy, and the breaking down of personal boundaries that always came with it.

As the car accelerated back into the outside lane, the screaming tension in his shoulders finally started to subside.

That moment of possessiveness, of connection between him and Ruby, had been nothing more than fatigue. They'd been up most of the night, spent several hours walking the Heath and then jumped straight back into bed for an encore as soon as they'd returned to his flat. When you factored in the long drive and the unsettling prospect of spending a weekend with his sister's family it was probably no wonder he'd let down his guard.

From now on he'd be more careful. And if he got curious about Ruby and her past again, he'd bite his damn tongue off before he gave in to the desire to know more.

CHAPTER ELEVEN

'GOOD GOD.' Ruby tilted her head back to gawk at Trewan Manor as Cal turned the car into the hedge-lined driveway.

With its towering gables and ramparts and the huge mullioned windows, the stone mansion looked like a cross between Cinderella's castle and the feverish imaginings of some mad Victorian architect. Ruby had first spotted the place as they wound their way up the coast road. Perched on the cliff, the gothic edifice looked dramatic and forbidding. But up close, Ruby noticed the welcoming touches—the flower-drenched boxes on the sills, the red glow of the dying sun sparkling on the sandstone, the fresh scent of sea salt and newly mown grass, and the Barbie scooter discarded on the front step—that turned the fairytale castle into a family home.

'How long has your sister lived here?' she asked as she stepped onto the gravel.

'Since she met Rye,' Cal remarked as he yanked their bags out of the back seat.

'And that would be when?' Ruby prompted.

'A few years ago.' He slammed the car's back door.

Ruby waited for him to say more. But he skirted the car in silence.

This was getting ridiculous. She'd dozed on and off throughout the journey, noticing each time she woke up that Cal seemed more and more tense and less and less talkative. She'd decided not to hold it against him, guessing he had to be as exhausted as she was after their all-nighter—and he'd had to do all the driving, because he was a tad precious about his new car. But honestly, what was the big secret?

'Are Maddy and her family part of a witness protection programme?' she asked, smiling sweetly as she held out her hand for her luggage. 'Because getting you to talk about them is harder than cracking the Enigma code.'

'Ha, ha,' he said, but still didn't elaborate.

Instead of handing Ruby her bag, he tucked

it under his arm, held his own and placed his free palm on the small of her back.

'I've got them,' he said, directing her towards the front door. 'Believe me, you're going to need both hands when you meet Maddy,' he added cryptically.

Ruby had only a moment to debate that before a slim young woman wearing a pair of denim cut-offs and a worn T-shirt burst through the front door. 'Cal, you made it.' Flinging her arms round Cal's neck, she bounced up on tiptoe and kissed his cheek. 'At last.'

'Hello, Maddy,' he said as she bounced back down and turned to Ruby. 'This is Ruby.'

'Ruby! This is fantastic,' she declared, grasping Ruby's hand in both of hers. 'It's great to meet you.'

The woman's eyes, the same striking emerald shade as Cal's, warmed with excitement and avid curiosity. 'I hope you didn't mind me strong-arming Cal into visiting. It's just Mia's really attached to him. And it's her birthday tomorrow.'

'That's absolutely fine,' Ruby said, feeling uncomfortable at Maddy's enthusiasm. It hadn't really occurred to her that they'd be deceiving Cal's sister by pretending to be a couple. The woman had greeted her as if she were someone significant, when she knew she wasn't.

'Where is Mia?' Cal asked.

'She crashed out about an hour ago. Thank goodness,' Maddy said as she led them into the house. 'When she heard you were definitely coming for her birthday she went into hyper-drive.' Maddy beamed at them both as she pushed open a door into a huge kitchen-dining room, which had a picture window that looked out onto the cliffs and bathed the room in natural light. 'Having her favourite uncle visit and a birthday party all in the same weekend is basically the definition of too much of a good thing for a three-year-old.'

'I'm her only uncle,' Cal remarked.

'Rye's checking on Mia,' Maddy said, ignoring the blunt comment. 'But I hope you haven't had supper yet. We held dinner for you.'

'No, we haven't,' Ruby answered when Cal remained silent. 'I know you weren't expecting me. I hope I'm not imposing.'

'Don't be silly. It's wonderful to have you here.' She waved the comment away. 'And I adore cooking. I'm sure Cal's told you I always make enough to feed a team of starving rugby players.' Crossing to the stove, she whipped a tray of flaky pastries out of the traditional Aga cooker.

The delicious scent of butter and spices and freshly cooked salmon had Ruby's stomach growling.

'That smells terrific,' she said, deciding not to divulge that Cal had mentioned virtually nothing about Maddy—except that she was deeply in love with her husband and her parents' disastrous marriage had been tough on her. Knowing something so personal about the woman and very little else made Ruby feel like even more of a fraud.

As Maddy arranged the pastries onto a plate and placed them on the large oak table Ruby noticed it was already laden with an impressive array of salads and appetisers. Her heart went out to her host. She'd gone to so much trouble—had probably spent most of the evening preparing the meal.

'What room are we in?' Cal asked. 'I'll go dump our stuff.'

'Oh, yes, of course,' Maddy said, sounding flustered now as she paused in the process of putting another place setting onto the table. 'I stuck you two doors down from Mia in the turret room. On the first floor. It's got a fantastic view of the bay.'

He nodded. 'Great.'

Ruby frowned as he walked out with the bags. Why was he being so stiff?

Maddy watched him go, her shoulders slumping slightly. 'I'm sorry, I should offer you a drink,' she said, shaking her head as if she'd momentarily forgotten Ruby was there. 'How does a glass of Pinot Grigio sound?' Maddy asked, her enthusiasm a little forced.

'Like a fantastic idea.' Ruby sent the other woman an encouraging smile, her empathy increasing. Men could be such morons. Especially men of the big-brother variety.

A little of the dancing light returned to Maddy's eyes. 'Come on, I've got a bottle in the fridge and some antipasti we can nibble on till the guys get back.'

They chatted about the trip down and the traffic out of London as Maddy uncorked the wine and poured Ruby a glass, then brought the promised plate of antipasti out of the fridge.

'Aren't you having a glass?' Ruby asked as she selected a stuffed mushroom from the lavish tray of home-made canapés.

Maddy's face flushed as she pressed a hand

to her midriff. 'I'm not drinking at the moment. Doctor's orders.'

Ruby swallowed. 'Oh, my goodness. Are you expecting a…?' She stopped abruptly, knowing she didn't have any right to ask such a personal question. She was only a stunt girlfriend, after all.

But Maddy just grinned and nodded. 'I haven't told Cal yet, so please don't say anything.'

'I won't,' Ruby said, feeling awkward again.

'Rye and I found out two weeks ago. It's one of the reasons I was so desperate to get Cal to come down this weekend. For once I didn't want to have to tell him something important over the phone.' Her voice literally bubbled with hope and enthusiasm. 'I hope you two didn't have too much planned—I assume you're the work he mentioned.'

'That would be me,' Ruby replied. Clearly Maddy wasn't quite as clueless about Cal's private life as he assumed.

Ruby toasted Maddy's invisible glass. 'Here's to the new uncle,' she said. 'I'm sure he's going to be thrilled,' she added.

Cal might be cynical about marriage, but

what man wouldn't be thrilled at becoming an uncle again?

Pouring herself a glass of soda water, Maddy clinked her glass to Ruby's. 'Let's hope so.' She took a long swallow and smacked her lips together. 'Not quite as good as Pinot Grigio, but it'll have to do for the next seven months.'

The cheerful comment sent a strange little dart of envy through Ruby. How odd. She wasn't broody. Not in the least. So where had that pang of longing come from?

Ruby pushed the confusing thought away as Cal walked back into the room accompanied by another man who approached her and offered his hand.

'Rye King, Maddy's husband. Welcome to Trewan Manor.'

With sunstreaked blond hair, a lean, athletic build effectively displayed beneath board shorts and a Hawaiian shirt and the sort of striking male beauty that could grace the cover of a glossy magazine, the man's uneven gait only added to his rugged, masculine appeal.

'Hi,' Ruby said, shaking his hand. Then recognition hit.

She actually had seen him on the cover of a

glossy magazine. A glossy business magazine to be precise. She'd read an article on the phenomenal growth of his sporting goods empire a few months ago. After re-reading it twice, she'd gained some useful tips about how to grow a fledgling idea from the ground up.

'King Xtreme,' she whispered in awe, naming the company he had founded after giving up a successful career as a champion surfer.

He ran his hand through his shaggy hair in a charmingly bashful gesture. 'Guilty as charged.'

'I was in one of your shops last week debating whether to buy a mountain bike.'

'So did we convince you?'

'I'm afraid there aren't enough mountains in Camden to justify letting me loose on an unsuspecting public.' She grinned at him. 'But I was very tempted.'

'I'll have to arrange a discount so we can tempt you more,' he said, slinging his arm around his wife's waist and nudging her hip against his.

The casually possessive gesture brought with it a poignant memory. How often had she seen her father hold her mother that way?

'Is Mia still asleep?' Maddy asked her husband.

'Are you joking? She's practically in a coma,' he said, leaning down to kiss his wife's hair. 'I'm betting we're going to get our first lie-in in three years tomorrow.'

'On her birthday?' Maddy laughed. 'How much do you want to bet?'

Ruby observed the conversation. Rye and Maddy's shared intimacy was a tangible demonstration of how much they loved and respected and desired each other.

The pang under her breastbone sharpened. And she studiously ignored it.

'Ruby happens to be lethal enough on four wheels,' Cal mentioned wryly as the four of them seated themselves round the table. 'So I wouldn't recommend trying to sell her a bike, Rye.'

'Hey, that accident was your fault, pal,' she said, glad to see that Cal seemed to have loosened up a little. 'My vehicle was stationary.'

'You two had an accident?' Maddy asked, passing the salads round.

'Not an accident. More like a fender-bender,' Ruby said. 'It's how we met yesterday,' she added slicing into the fragrant pastry. Her fork stopped halfway to her mouth when she saw Maddy's eyes widen to saucer size.

'You only met yesterday?'

Ruby felt the blush stain her neck. Oops. Looked as if she'd blown her stunt girlfriend cover. She lowered her fork. 'Actually, yes.'

She heard a low groan from Cal but refused to look at him. She'd never agreed to lie. And having met Maddy, she was glad the other woman knew the truth. Cal's sister was warm, generous and remarkably friendly and she wouldn't feel right pretending to mean more to Cal than she did.

'But that's terrific!' Maddy laughed. 'You only met my brother yesterday and yet he brought you down with him.' She handed Ruby the salad bowl. 'You two must have really hit it off.'

Cal coughed strategically. 'Maddy, do me a favour and don't start picking out the wedding china just yet.'

'But, Cal, you've got to admit this is significant.' She patted Cal's cheek, obviously enjoying teasing him. 'Ruby's the first woman you've agreed to spend six hours in a car with. Which means you must have actually talked to her.'

Ruby relaxed, intrigued by the mention of Cal's love life and amused by his sister's assessment.

Maddy sent Ruby a conspiratorial wink. 'I

think it's great. Do you know you're the first girlfriend he's ever brought to meet us?'

Cal scowled over his dinner and Ruby felt the swell of pleasure. He'd been her first one-night stand, it was good to know she'd have some significance for him too when they parted. She smiled at Maddy. 'So how many girlfriends has Cal had?'

'Billions, I'm afraid,' Maddy responded playfully. 'But I'm sure he's never had a proper conversation with any of them. Until you.'

'Do you two mind? I'm sitting right here,' Cal announced grumpily.

'I know you are…' Maddy swivelled round to face her brother, the teasing smile disappearing. 'And for the first time in six months. Despite my endless invites. Why is that?'

Ruby had to give Cal's sister credit, it was a neatly delivered non sequitur.

Cal gave a tense shrug. 'I've been busy.'

'So you say.' Maddy sighed.

Rye covered his wife's hand. 'Why don't you tell Cal the news, now you've managed to get him here?' he said, lightly.

If he was trying to distract his wife, it worked. Maddy gripped his fingers, her smile returning full force.

'What news?' Cal asked, sounding wary.

Maddy rested a hand on her midriff, her face beaming with that fierce combination of pride and hope that had captivated Ruby in the kitchen. 'You're going to be an uncle again.'

Instead of looking pleased, Cal's expression barely changed. 'I see.'

There was a short silence, then Maddy gave a hollow laugh. 'Is that all you have to say?'

He put down his knife and fork. 'I suppose congratulations are in order.'

If Ruby had ever heard of a more grudging congratulations she couldn't think of one.

'You *suppose*?' Although masked by annoyance, the hurt and confusion in Maddy's voice were clear. Ruby stared, astonished at Cal's lukewarm reaction. It was almost as if he wasn't happy about the news.

'When's the baby due?' Ruby interrupted, hoping to cut through the tension as Cal simply stared at his sister. That his usual articulacy had completed deserted him also seemed significant.

Maddy gathered herself, forcing the smile back in place. 'By our calculation, it's due in about seven months. Which will make it a spring baby.'

'Have you told Mia yet?'

Maddy shook her head, blinking away the suspicious sheen in her eyes. 'No, not yet,' she said dully.

'We're not kidding ourselves,' Rye added, helping Ruby out. 'Mia's going to love the idea of a baby brother or sister, but once they start playing with her toys we're going to have World War Three on our hands. At the moment Mia's king of the hill around here and boy does she know it.'

'I can't wait to meet her,' Ruby said and meant it. She'd always adored children; they were endlessly fascinating and at Mia's age impossibly cute. And Mia sounded like quite a character.

She and Rye continued to talk about the new arrival, with Maddy bolstering herself and joining in, but Cal remained stonily silent. As the meal ended Maddy excused herself, pleading exhaustion due to her pregnancy. She didn't fool Ruby, who had been painfully aware of the young woman's attempts to get Cal back into the conversation.

Ruby helped Rye clear away the dishes while Cal loaded the dishwasher. Then she bid Rye goodnight. Cal fell into step beside her.

'Wait up, Cal. I need a word,' Rye called after them.

'Sure,' he said, apparently unaware of the sharp note Ruby had detected in Rye's request.

She watched the two men walk into the front parlour in silence. As she mounted the stairs to the landing she wondered about the rift between Cal and his sister. Surely Maddy's tendency to matchmake couldn't be the cause of Cal's prickly demeanor tonight. It had to be more than that. Why his behaviour should make her feel weary and dispirited, she had no idea.

'What the hell is your problem, pal?'

Irritation stirred in Cal's stomach as his brother-in-law glared at him.

He was tired, confused and for some inexplicable reason his emotions were much closer to the surface than usual. This was the last thing he needed.

'I didn't have a problem,' he said. 'Until now.'

As he turned to leave Rye grabbed hold of his arm and yanked him back. 'My wife spent three hours cooking dinner tonight. She wanted to make this special. For you.' Rye gave him a derogatory look. 'Because you're important to her. Although I can't imagine why, because it's pretty obvious she's not important to you.'

Cal's temper snapped as the guilt he always kept strictly leashed flared to life. He pulled his arm out of Rye's grasp. 'Back off. My relationship with my sister is none of your business.'

Rye gave a harsh laugh. 'Think again. She's my *wife*. I'm the one has to watch her fight to hold the tears back when you say you're coming and don't show. Or give her some stupid excuse why you can't make it at the last minute. Do you have any idea how much that hurts her, knowing you don't give a damn about her?'

The dart hit home, but Cal refused to let it show on his face, his expression rigid. 'It was never my intention to hurt her.'

Rye's eyes narrowed, then his brows rose. 'Damn. You really don't get it, do you?'

'Get what?'

'That she's never going to stop caring about you. Maddy's not made that way. She never gives up on people—even you.'

'Thanks for the lecture. I'll bear it in mind.' Cal turned to walk away, an emotion burning in his chest that he didn't recognise or understand. He never lost control, because he'd spent so much of his childhood despising his parents for always losing theirs. But when Maddy had told him about the new baby, he'd been frozen in place, unable to congratulate her, unable to voice his joy at her announcement—or deal with the crushing sense of inadequacy. Maddy had always asked so little of him. So why did he feel incapable of giving her even this much?

As he opened the door Rye's parting shot stopped him dead. 'Don't hurt my wife again. Or I'll hurt you.'

It was an empty threat. Maddy would be devastated if her husband and her brother came to blows and Rye had to know that. But even so, Cal glanced back. Seeing the anger and the turmoil in Rye's face, he was forced to acknowledge the truth.

Rye was right. His sister wasn't going to let him go, however much he might want her to.

He gave a stiff nod. 'I'll talk to her tomorrow.'

CHAPTER TWELVE

ENTERING the large attic bedroom, Cal came to an abrupt halt as he spotted Ruby on the opposite side of the room. The sight of her sitting in the window seat, her legs curled under her and her head buried in a paperback novel was so unexpected and so beguiling, it momentarily wiped the ugly scene with Rye from his mind.

With her riotous hair tied back, her face scrubbed clean and a pair of spectacles perched on her nose, she could easily have been mistaken for a solemn, thoughtful schoolgirl.

An unsettling picture formed in his mind of her as a child, valiantly struggling to cope with her mother's death and her brother's rejection—and was swiftly followed by the feeling of hopelessness and futility that had dogged him throughout his own childhood.

But then his gaze dipped, and he took in the outline of her nipples through the sheer material of her nightgown.

The familiar pulse of heat had him shaking off the thought as he crossed the room. Any common ground he and Ruby shared was cosmetic and purely coincidental.

And the problem at the moment wasn't her family. It was his.

He hadn't set out to hurt his sister, but he had. Which meant he'd have to figure out a way to apologise tomorrow. Not a conversation he was looking forward to.

'At last, we're finally alone,' he said, tension tightening his shoulders as he kicked off his loafers and lay down on the wide bed.

Ruby's head lifted. She took her glasses off and put her book down. Slipping the band out of her hair, she shook out the mass of curls as she stepped off the window seat. As if by magic, any traces of the studious little girl disappeared and she evolved into the voluptuous take-no-prisoners virago he had come to know.

Cal heaved out a sigh as he watched her stroll towards him, the muscles in his shoulders beginning to loosen as he took in the seductive sway of her hips and the way the nightgown slid over her curves. A new, more sublime tension tightened his groin.

Thank God he'd brought her along. Sinking into Ruby's lush, responsive body was the perfect way to forget the ordeal he had in store for tomorrow.

'Come here.' He patted the mattress, then folded his arms behind his head and fixed his gaze on the fascinating glimpse of cleavage displayed by her wispy nightgown. 'And prepare to be ravished for the rest of the night.'

She gave a throaty laugh. 'Forget it,' she purred. 'No ravishing allowed tonight.'

He grasped her wrist, tugged her on top of him. 'Stop playing hard to get.'

She laughed again, but drew back. 'I'm serious. We're not making love when there's a three-year-old sleeping down the hall.'

His shoulders tensed right back up again. 'Since when did you become a prude?'

She smiled that superior smile that women only ever used when a guy was desperate. 'Ever since you turned me into a screamer.'

There was that.

He let her go. Frustration making the muscles in his neck bunch.

Terrific.

This trip kept getting better and better.

Swinging his legs to the floor, he ploughed his fingers through his hair. 'We should never have come,' he growled, to no one in particular. 'I knew it would be a disaster.'

'What exactly is the problem with your sister?'

Cal looked over his shoulder. 'Huh?'

'Why did you react that way when she told you about the baby?'

He groaned. 'I'm tired. It's been a long day. Can we talk about this another time?' *Like never.*

'But you were so—'

'Look, Ruby,' he interrupted sharply. 'You're here because we amuse each other in bed, not to make observations about my family relations.'

She flinched as if she'd been struck. 'Gee, thanks, Cal.' She got off the bed, glared down at him. 'Perhaps I should just tattoo "Cal's Tart" to my forehead, so I don't get confused.'

He stood up and grabbed hold of her waist. 'Don't get upset,' he said, feeling like a heel. He'd seen the hurt in her eyes, right alongside the temper. 'I shouldn't have said that. I don't think of you as my tart. That's not what I meant.'

She pulled free. 'So what did you mean?' she snapped, not sounding all that forgiving. Who could blame her? He'd made a mess of things. This was getting to be a habit.

'Nothing,' he said wearily. He sank back onto the bed, raked his fingers through his hair, the frustration starting to choke him. He was usually so eloquent with words. He made a living from advocacy, from being erudite and compelling when he was addressing a jury, or outlining a mitigation plea to a judge. Why couldn't he say a single thing right tonight?

'I'm afraid you'll have to do better than that,' she said, her hands now perched on her hips. The stance was combative, but the fire in her eyes had dimmed.

He blew out a breath. He'd expected tears or a tantrum. He had to be grateful he'd got neither. 'I guess I'm feeling kind of tense tonight,' he said grudgingly. 'And I took it out on you.'

She didn't look mad any more, she looked intrigued. Somehow he wasn't sure that was necessarily a good thing. 'Why does their happiness make you so uncomfortable?'

'What?' he croaked. *Where had that come from?*

'You said yourself you were tense. And the way you reacted when Maddy told you about the...' She paused, her eyes lighting with knowledge. 'You feel excluded. Is that it?'

'Excluded?' Why the hell would he feel excluded? Rye and Maddy had the exact opposite of what he wanted out of life. 'From what exactly?' he said, the tension starting to band around his temples now like a vice.

'Because they love each other. You feel left out.'

'Give me a break,' he scoffed. 'What does that even mean? Love's just a word people use to justify lust or dependency or both,' he said.

'That's ridiculous. How can you say that? Haven't you ever been in love?' She looked even more astonished, but what annoyed him was the distinct note of pity.

'Are you telling me you have?' he countered.

'Of course, I have.'

'Who with? Who have you been in love with?' he challenged. What kind of guy would be able to trick Ruby into thinking she was in love?

'What? Do you want a list or something?'

'Yeah, I guess I do,' he said, surprised by the twinge of jealousy.

'All right, then. Fine.' She plopped down on the bed and crossed her legs. 'Jackson Dalton was my first love. He lived across the road from us and had these dreamy brown eyes and incredibly cool dreadlocks. And...'

'You see, that's lust, pure and simple. You fancied this Jackson guy.' Like all women, Ruby had fallen into the trap of thinking her baser instincts had to be justified by purer, more altruistic emotions.

She cocked an eyebrow. 'So suddenly now you're an expert?'

'I'm just stating the—'

'Yeah, I know what you were just stating, Westmore. Get your mind out of the gutter. I was eleven. At that age even I didn't know about the joys of sex. He walked me home every day after school. He told me about how he was going to play for Spurs and I told him all about my plans to open the best Italian restaurant in London. We never even kissed. It was the least lust-inspired love affair I ever had.'

'What you're talking about is puppy love.' He thrust a finger at her. 'Where's Jackson now if he was so important to you?'

She grasped his finger. 'Quit cross-examining me, barrister. He moved to Manchester when I was twelve.'

'How convenient,' he said.

'God, Westmore. Cynical, much?' She huffed. 'Are you seriously telling me you never loved any of your girlfriends? Ever? How is that possible? According to your sister you've had billions.'

'Billions is a slight exaggeration,' he said laconically. 'But I can safely say, I have never been in love and I intend to make damn sure I never will be.'

She didn't say anything for the longest time. 'Cal,' she whispered. 'That's the saddest thing I've ever heard.' The sympathy in her eyes made him stiffen. 'Why not? Why wouldn't you want that in your life? To have a connection with another human being that matters? How can you reject out of hand the one thing in human existence that can make you feel fantastic and doesn't cost a thing?'

'Doesn't cost a thing?' he sneered, the bitterness he'd thought he'd buried years before scolding his throat. 'It costs plenty. What about pride and dignity and self-respect?'

* * *

Wow, someone had really done a number on him. That was the only explanation, Ruby thought sadly. How could anyone want to close themselves off from all the wonderful things that went with falling in love?

The companionship, the sense of connection, the sweet comfort of familiarity and routine when you'd been dating someone for a while. Of course, there was usually a price to pay when you fell out of love again, she thought, remembering the sense of failure when she'd finally had to admit to herself that Johnny, like Ty, her teenage boyfriend, and even her first love Jackson before him, wasn't the one after all. It had hurt, but that cruel moment of disillusionment and disappointment had never been anywhere near as bad as the wrenching pain of losing her mother or her brother.

'Who was she?' she asked, unaccountably angry with this unknown woman.

'Who was who?'

'The woman who destroyed your faith in relationships?'

His brows lowered, his confusion clear. 'There wasn't a woman. I told you, I don't fall in love. That's for fools and romantics. I'm neither.'

The flat defensive tone tugged at something deep inside Ruby. The hard expression on Cal's face reminded her of Nick, and all those times she'd seen him try to hide his hurt and vulnerability behind a scowl.

She pressed her palm to his cheek, sympathy for him overwhelming her. 'Cal, there has to be a reason why you don't trust anyone. Is this something to do with your parents—and the disastrous marriage you told me about? Is that why you're so cynical?'

He drew back. 'It's not cynicism. It's realism,' he said, the bitterness making his eyes glitter. 'They put Maddy through hell with their constant rows and reconciliations.'

'And they put you through hell too.'

'No, they didn't. Because I knew their marriage was a sham. I knew he couldn't keep his dick in his pants. That he made promises he couldn't keep.'

'How did you know?'

'Because I was his alibi.'

'His what?'

'His alibi.' Cal pushed the words out past the hot ball of resentment and disgust. 'Every Saturday morning, he told my mother he was taking me to a judo class. Then he'd go bang one of his mistresses, while I sat outside in the car.'

'He took you with him?' The look of horror that crossed Ruby's face had guilty knowledge clawing up his throat. He swallowed it down. He'd got over that years ago.

'But that's appalling,' she said.

'Yeah, well… It certainly opened my eyes to the sanctity of marriage. And the truth about true love. That it doesn't exist.'

He gave a grim laugh. As a kid, he'd always wanted to tell someone. So he could stop it somehow, but he'd never had the guts. How pathetic that he should finally break his silence when it couldn't make any difference any more.

'Cal, that's dreadful. What did you do?'

He heard the outrage in her voice and wondered who it was for.

'I kept my mouth shut.' He could still remember the sting across his cheek of the back-hander his father had given him when he'd threatened to tell. He'd got over the urge pretty quickly. 'It wasn't so dreadful,' he added dryly. 'I was never a big fan of judo.'

'How long did it go on?'

He shrugged. 'I can't remember.'

Had it been a year? Two? However long

it had been, it had felt like for ever at the time. Being trapped in a lie he had no control over. He could still remember the fear every Saturday, the terror that his mother and Maddy would find out. And the way the fear had curdled in his stomach, until it had turned into a lead weight of loathing. By the end of it, he had a knowledge of adult relationships he didn't want and had despised both his parents. His father for the lies and the cheating, and his mother for her weakness in never facing the truth. He'd promised himself he'd never get into that situation again. Forced to protect something that wasn't even real.

'Did he eventually stop?' Ruby asked, the hopeful question making him bark out a hollow laugh.

'No, she eventually found out. They had a row and she kicked him out.' He paused trying to blank the memory of their angry shouts and Maddy's gulping sobs. 'She took him back again a few weeks later.' And it had started all over again. 'Because, you see, she *loved* him.'

He could hear the cynical edge in the words.

Ruby stared at him, the combination of warmth and understanding in her eyes making him desperately uncomfortable. Why was she looking at him as if any of this mattered?

'No wonder you don't believe in love,' she murmured at last.

He wanted to say I told you so. But somehow the words wouldn't come, because instead of acquiescence he saw defeat in her face.

'Let's go to bed,' he said, deliberately changing the subject. 'I'm shattered.'

'You look it,' she said, then threaded her fingers into his hair and tugged his mouth down to hers.

The kiss was soft, tender, but had hunger coiling in his gut. 'I guess we both need some sleep,' she whispered.

She was probably right. He *was* tired. So tired he could feel his bones melting as he kicked off his trousers and settled onto the bed beside her.

He took a deep breath of her sultry vanilla scent but kept his hands to himself. She snuggled against him, her bottom brushing over the erection.

He hissed out a breath as blood pounded into his groin.

'Stop torturing me and lie still,' he growled, anchoring her to him when she wriggled again. But then his arm brushed against the swell of her breast, and he captured the warm flesh in his palm without thinking, outlining the hard bud of her nipple through the silky fabric of her nightgown.

'It's okay, Cal,' she murmured softly. 'Sometimes losing yourself in sex helps. Maybe if we're careful…'

He didn't need to lose himself. What was she talking about? But he felt as if he were teetering on a high ledge, the urge to leap off overwhelming him.

To hell with this.

He ran his free hand up her thigh, found her naked bottom beneath the thin gown. 'You'll just have to keep the noise down,' he murmured, nipping her ear lobe as he massaged the plump, downy skin.

She gave a soft groan and rolled onto her back. 'I'm not sure I can be quiet with you,' she whispered, brushing her fingers across the cotton of his boxers.

He gritted his teeth, her clever touch torturing him. Then gave a low groan as his fingers found the wet, swollen folds of her sex.

His breath rasped out as he stroked and circled the nub of her clitoris with his thumb.

She stiffened, moaned, spurring on the hunger, the need.

'Don't come,' he said. 'Not yet.' He had to be inside her, the demand clutching at his gut like a wild beast as he levered himself up, settled over her. Dragging off her nightgown, he flung it aside. 'Are you on the pill? I'm safe.'

She nodded, her eyes wide.

Thank God. He couldn't stop, couldn't take the time to find the damn condoms and put one on.

Clutching her hips, forcing her legs wide, he impaled her in one long, solid stroke. She sobbed, bit her lip, as her sex clenched and released, then tightened around him.

He established a rhythm, pressing his hand to her mouth to catch her muffled scream as she arched under him, her muscles convulsing as she came. He struggled to cling on, to keep a stranglehold on the need, but then the last thin thread snapped. The vicious orgasm slammed into him with the unstoppable force of a runaway train—hard and fast and explosive.

Cal waited for his heartbeat to ease out of the danger zone.

'I should have used a condom,' he murmured, feeling dazed and embarrassed. What had just come over him? Where had that all-consuming need come from? And why hadn't he been able to control it?

Her chin lifted, those dark eyes steady on his as she flattened her palm against his chest. 'I'm safe. I've never done it without proper protection before.'

The practicality had his heartbeat slowing a little.

He covered her hand. 'Me neither.'

She yawned, cradling her head on his shoulder. 'I guess that's another first for us both, then,' she said, her voice thick with fatigue. The murmured observation made his blood pressure shoot back up as her body relaxed into sleep.

Pulling up the sheet to cover them both, he smoothed it over her lush figure with unsteady hands and gazed out of the window. A million stars winked back at him, their brilliance lighting up the night sky as they never did in London. Unfortunately they failed to illuminate the events of the last twenty minutes.

Why the hell had he done that? Confiding the sordid details of his parents' marriage? And where had that frantic desire to possess her come from? He'd never taken a woman without a condom before—but not just for personal safety reasons. He'd never trusted one before enough to risk the possibility of an unplanned pregnancy.

She shifted against his side, and he stared at the top of her head, the rich red-brown curls glossy in the moonlight. So what had made him so sure he could trust Ruby?

He eased out a careful breath.

All right, fatigue was making him crazy. Ruby was smart, and he knew how much her business meant to her. She was far too intelligent, far too focused to risk an unplanned pregnancy. That was how he knew he could trust her.

But as he listened to the gentle murmur of her breathing his heartbeat continued to hammer in his throat. Trusting Ruby not to lie about birth control was one thing, losing control of himself like that quite another.

He pressed his hand to his chest. She'd got to him somehow, he thought wearily as he willed himself to drift into a fitful sleep.

He'd have to make sure it didn't happen again.

CHAPTER THIRTEEN

'Now, we can have pink icing or blue,' Ruby offered, whipping the butter into a creamy mass. 'What do you reckon, Mia?'

'Pink!' The little girl bounced onto her toes and clapped her hands.

Ruby added the drops of colouring to the mix as Maddy rushed into the room trailing a bunch of balloons.

'Thanks so much for doing this.' Maddy riffled through the kitchen drawers. 'There it is.' She held a roll of ribbon aloft. Plopping into one of the kitchen chairs, she began threading the ribbon through the bunch of balloons. 'That cake smells delicious.'

'Good.' Ruby smiled, handing Mia the punnet of fresh strawberries they'd washed and hulked together. 'I need you to pick out your favourites, Mia, because only the very best can end up on a birthday cake.'

The child stopped bouncing and held the punnet as if she had been given the crown jewels. 'Yes, Miss Ruby.'

Ruby smiled, her heart melting. According to Maddy, Mia had started nursery a few weeks ago and had got into the habit of calling everyone Miss. It was just one more adorable thing about the toddler. Her live-wire chatter, her cherubic face, the bright green eyes and cap of soft blond curls were a few others. Ruby could see why any mother would forgive her for waking at the crack of dawn that morning.

Leaving Cal sound asleep upstairs over an hour ago, Ruby had pitched in to help when she'd seen how exhausted both Rye and Maddy were after their early-morning wake-up call—and how much they still had to do to be ready for their daughter's party at noon. Plus she'd needed something to do, to take her mind off the peculiar way her heart had leapt into her throat when she'd woken up to find herself cradled in Cal's arms.

'Tell me again how many children you have coming,' Ruby asked as she swirled the buttercream icing onto the sponge base while her pint-size sous chef plucked strawberries out of the punnet as if she were prospecting for gold.

Maddy sent her a flustered grin. 'I'm not sure. All Mia's friends have older or younger siblings and it felt mean not to invite them too. And...' she threw up her hands in desperation '...basically I think we have half of Cornwall's under-fives on the guest list.'

Ruby shook her head, laughing. 'It's official. Both you and Rye are completely insane.'

'I thought I had everything under control. But somehow things just sneak up on you. I still can't believe I forgot the cake.'

'I can,' Ruby said, marvelling anew at how Maddy could even remember her own name amidst the chaos. Finishing the final swirl of the icing, she placed the cake in front of Mia. 'Do you want to add the strawberries?'

'Can I?' Mia said with a reverential breath.

'Whose cake is it?'

'My cake,' Mia piped.

'Well, then, I guess that's okay.'

Mia gave a little hoot and began carefully placing the strawberries on top.

'You're marvellous with her,' Maddy said. 'And that cake is awesome. When you have kids of your own, their friends are going to be begging for party invitations.'

'Thanks.' Ruby brushed off the compliment despite the pang kicking her ribs again. She hadn't given it a lot of thought. But she couldn't imagine children being on the horizon any time soon. Why should the thought make her life feel empty all of a sudden?

She heard a loud sniff from behind her, and glanced round to see a tear slip down Maddy's cheek. 'Is everything all right?'

'Ignore me.' Maddy huffed as she whipped a tissue out of the pocket of her shorts. 'It's the pregnancy hormones, they turn me into a basket case.' She blew her nose loudly, brushed away the trickle of tears. 'I'm just so happy Cal's finally found someone like you.'

'Oh.' Ruby's smile faltered. 'We're not exactly...' She paused, not wanting to ruin Maddy's happy grin. 'We've only known each other a few days. It's nothing serious.'

'I know, I know.' Maddy waved the tissue. 'I'm letting what Cal likes to call my hopeless romantic gene get ahead of itself and probably scaring the life out of you. And I'm sure Cal would throttle me if he heard me saying this. But you're so perfect for him. It's hard not to hope for the best for the two of you.'

Ruby gave a half-smile, her heart gallop-
ing into her throat, and had absolutely no idea
what to say. Maddy really was a hopeless romantic. The very idea that Ruby was perfect
for anyone seemed a little absurd. But perfect
for Cal? She doubted that.

The tiny glimpse she'd got last night of
the man behind the confident, charismatic
charmer had touched her deeply. Her heart
had gone out to that vulnerable little boy,
forced to keep such a hideous secret for so
long. She'd wanted to reach out to him. To
somehow make it right. To break through that
cast-iron control that she now suspected was
a result of a desperately insecure childhood.

Then when he'd made love to her, with a
raw passion that had consumed them both, for
a few blissful moments of afterglow she'd de-
luded herself into believing it had been more
than just sex.

But as she'd lain awake beside him this
morning, watching him sleeping, those long
lashes touching chiselled cheeks and making
him look young and boyish, she'd realised
how ludicrous that was—and had pulled herself back from the brink.

Cal would probably want to throttle her too
if he could have heard the soft, fluffy direction

of her thoughts. Both of them were perfectly clear this was a one-weekend fling. Nothing more or less. The idea that he had needed her in some elemental way had simply been a figment of her overactive imagination.

'I don't understand him at all, you know,' Maddy said, the wistful note in her voice making Ruby's heart skitter in her chest. This was not a conversation she needed to be having right now. Trying to figure Cal out was what had made her so delusional last night.

'Men make it their mission in life to be completely obtuse. Cal's just like the rest of his breed,' Ruby replied, trying for flippant. And not quite pulling it off.

'I don't understand why he's always tried to distance himself from me and my family,' Maddy continued. 'And why he never gets close to the women he dates. I think it has something to do with Mum and Dad and the constant rows, but he won't admit it.'

'How do you mean?' It was a leading question, which Ruby knew she ought to take back the minute it popped out of her mouth. She shouldn't be encouraging this. Callum Westmore was a glorified one-night stand. The man and his past and the complex emotions he had stirred in her last night were better left alone.

'Cal says he doesn't believe in love. That it doesn't exist.' Maddy sighed. 'But I don't think that's true. It's not that he doesn't believe in love. It's that he doesn't trust it. Or rather he's scared to trust it. Because if he did he's convinced he'd end up in the sort of misery our parents called a marriage.'

'From what Cal's told me, it doesn't sound like your parents ever loved each other.'

'They didn't.' Maddy's eyes rounded. 'He's talked to you about them?'

Ruby blanched, knowing she'd overstepped another line. 'Only a little bit.'

'That's amazing.' Maddy's face lit with fierce approval. 'A bit's more than he's ever been willing to share with me.' She took a deep breath, clearly eager to say more, when her gaze shifted and she shot off her chair. 'Mia, what are you doing?'

'I love strawbrees, Mummy,' Mia said owlishly, her face and hands covered in the juicy red stains of her crimes.

'I know, but you weren't supposed to eat them all, sweetie. Not yet.'

Ruby chuckled, pushing aside the let-down feeling as she helped Maddy clean up the mess. She'd been eager to hear more about Cal, which could not be good. She shouldn't want to know more; her curiosity had got her into enough trouble already.

As Maddy scooped up her daughter the little girl squealed and wriggled furiously stretching out her arms. 'Uncle Cal. My uncle Cal.'

Ruby watched as Maddy put the toddler down and the child raced across the kitchen as fast as her solid little legs would carry her.

'Hey there, Mia. How's the birthday girl?' Cal lowered onto one knee, awkwardly catching his niece as she barrelled into him and threw her arms around his neck.

As Mia babbled away he sent the little girl a crooked smile and brushed her hair back. But when she buried her face in his neck and he lifted her into his arms, his gaze flashed to Ruby.

The emerald green glinted with something dark and dangerous, the line of his jaw rigid with tension.

Ruby swallowed. Exactly how long had he been standing in that doorway?

'I'll be back in a minute, Mia,' he said, passing the child to her mother. 'I won't be long, I promise. But I have to talk to my friend

Ruby first.' The frigid anger in his tone had heat prickling the back of Ruby's neck and rising up her scalp. 'In private.'

CHAPTER FOURTEEN

'You can let go of my arm now. I'm not going to run away,' Ruby said with strained patience as she was hauled down the last few stone steps to the beach.

Cal hadn't said a word as he'd propelled her out of the back door of the house, then marched her down the cliff path. And she'd put up with it. Clearly he was a little miffed about whatever he'd overheard. He'd obviously walked in on her talking with Maddy and he wasn't too pleased about them discussing him.

But any guilt Ruby had felt about her curiosity was fast being washed away on a tidal wave of annoyance.

Finally releasing her arm, Cal strode ahead, then stopped and braced his feet apart. From the rigid line of his shoulders she suspected miffed might be a bit of an understatement.

He remained silent, his back to her as the wind whipped her cheeks and the quiet rush of the surf covered the unsteady beat of her heart.

'So what exactly is it that you were so desperate to talk to me about?' she goaded, unable to wait meekly for the explosion she suspected was coming. She didn't like being ordered about. By anyone.

The vicious swear word echoed away on the wind. She flinched as he swung back round and strode towards her. 'Don't *ever* talk to my sister about me again,' he said, his face thunderous as he towered over her.

She crossed her arms over her chest, let the indignation stiffen her backbone. Maybe he had a right to be a little annoyed, but this was totally out of order. 'Don't bully me, Cal,' she said, refusing to be cowed by him, or his temper.

'Bully you?' He stepped closer, gripped her chin between his thumb and forefinger, forcing her to face the full power of his glare. 'What I want to do is bend you over my knee and spank you, so believe me, you're getting off lightly.'

Ruthlessly quashing the dark thrill that shot through her at the passion in his words—that definitely was not appropriate—Ruby twisted her head out of his grasp. 'And there I was thinking you were far too upright to consider sado-masochism as a lifestyle choice.'

'This isn't a bloody joke,' he snarled, her attempt to break the tension falling spectacularly flat. 'How much did you tell her?'

The words sliced out, volatile with temper. The veneer of logic, of civilised behaviour had been torn away. Ruby struggled to make sense of the sudden firestorm, trying to quell the wild beat of her heart and the sizzle of awareness that arched between them like an electric current.

What on earth was he so upset about?

'Tell her about what?'

'About what I told you last night. About what I knew. About my father and his mistresses.' He hurled the words at her, but what she saw in his eyes right alongside the anger shocked her more. Panic.

Her heart squeezed in her chest, the rush of tenderness painful in its intensity. 'You never told Maddy?'

'Of course not.'

'Why not?'

He turned his back on the question, sank his fists into the pockets of his shorts. His body vibrated with tension. 'What the hell was I thinking spilling my guts like that?' he muttered, more to himself than her. 'I must have lost my mind.'

'I didn't tell her, Cal.' Stepping forward, she placed her palm on his back. The urge to touch him, to soothe, overwhelming her. 'But you should.'

She felt the muscles on his spine tense.

He gave a brittle laugh as he turned, dislodging her hand. 'You don't know what you're talking about.'

'Cal, how can you think any of that was your fault?'

Why was he being so hard on himself?

'Maddy caught him banging his secretary when she was fourteen years old and it nearly destroyed her,' he shouted. 'That's on me. If I'd been able to stop him. If I'd told my mother. If I'd at least let Maddy know what he was really like.'

'It's not on you,' she shouted back. 'Can't you see, whatever you did or didn't do wouldn't have made any difference? Some things you can't control, no matter how much you might want to. You have to tell her, Cal.'

The sharp frown of frustration arrowed down. 'I'm not telling her and neither are you.

It will only open up old wounds which have healed.'

'How could they be healed, when you're cutting yourself off from the only family you have?'

'I'm not talking about me. I don't have any wounds. I'm talking about Maddy.'

How could he be so clever with words, so smart and analytical, and yet such a dolt when it came to the simplest of relationships?

He did have wounds. And ones that went much deeper than Maddy's, she suspected.

'Maddy's much tougher than you think,' she said, trying to approach the problem from a different angle. 'You don't have to protect her.'

'And you know this from what? One ten-minute conversation with her?' he snarled. 'I think I know my sister better than you do.'

Ruby ignored the sneering contempt in his voice. He was still angry, still raw.

'How can you know her?' she shot right back. 'When you refuse to even talk to her properly?' She dragged in a breath, determined to hammer her point home. 'She's a strong, capable woman who's building a home here. Building a loving relationship. Building a life that matters. If you're so well adjusted, why are you so scared to be a part of it?'

'I'm not scared. I just don't want to be part of it,' he said, the frustration making a muscle bunch in his cheek.

'Of course you do.'

He swore loudly. 'Do you have any idea how ridiculous that sounds coming from you? If you really think home and family are so wonderful, why haven't you built the same thing for yourself?'

The snarled question had her opening her mouth. Then closing it again.

She wrapped her arms around her waist, the salty wind tearing at her hair and stinging her cheeks as the strike hit home. 'This isn't about me,' she said, trying for measured and reasonable, even though her insides were boiling, her heart burning. 'This is about you and—'

'We're through talking.' He grasped her arms, hauled her up on tiptoes. 'This conversation is over.'

His lips crushed hers, the kiss ruthless, and demanding but so full of desperation, and heat, Ruby felt the response right down to her toes.

Her head told her to push him away, not to

surrender to his attempt to silence her. But her heart and her hormones screamed something entirely different.

Wrestling her arms free, Ruby thrust her hands into his hair and opened her mouth, letting the rush of heat consume them both. She fed on his passion, his anger, pressed against the solid weight of his arousal—meeting the unstoppable force of his will with the immoveable object of her desire.

She had no doubt he'd meant to punish her with the kiss, but when he finally lifted his head, he looked stunned and aroused, but the storm of aggression had passed.

'Why can't you ever do what you're told?' he murmured as he touched his forehead to hers, the rigidity of his shoulders softening as his hands caressed her bottom.

She was fairly sure it was a rhetorical question but she answered it anyway. 'Because that would be incredibly boring.'

He gave a harsh laugh. 'That's one shortcoming no one could ever accuse you of.'

The unspoken suggestion that there were several other shortcomings he could accuse her of stung a little, but Ruby let it pass. She cupped his cheeks, met his eyes. 'Tell her, Cal. Don't let it fester any longer.' She thought of her own family and the secret that had eventually torn them apart. 'Believe me, secrets are never a good idea.'

He gave a heavy sigh, pulled back. 'I'll take it under advisement,' he said.

It was a concession. A compromise. Maybe he would finally talk to Maddy, let her into his life. And maybe he wouldn't. But she'd done her best. She had to leave it at that.

She stepped back too, let his hands drop from her hips, suddenly wary of the intensity of her own emotions. There was something disturbing about the yearning to help, to resolve, to understand this hard, indomitable man that was still lodged in her chest.

She'd led with her heart, and she refused to regret that, but now she needed to use her head. And back off. For her own protection.

'Good.' She pushed her hair out of her eyes, let the wind whip the errant strands away from her face. 'You do that,' she said, feeling desperately exposed all of a sudden. And more than a little awkward.

He brushed a knuckle across her cheek, rubbed his thumb across her lip. 'I don't suppose there's any chance of a quickie on the beach? To kiss and make up properly.'

The cheeky suggestion was intended to

break the mood, but it still had her heart beating double time in her chest. 'I'm afraid I promised to make cupcakes to go with the cake,' she said, determined to ignore the emotion clogging her throat. 'And I have a rule against doing anything that would risk getting sand in places I may find it hard to get it out of again.'

He smiled, and made her heartbeat peak painfully.

Remember, Ruby, this is not a real relationship. And you don't want it to be.

She fluttered her eyelashes, wiggled her brows salaciously. 'But we can certainly take a rain check. As long as you remember to bring your gag,' she added, trying her best to lighten the mood too.

Sex was simple—the one thing she could offer him without complications. And it was the only reason she was really here.

He chuckled, the sound gruff with desire and appreciation. Basking in his approval had been wonderful once, but that too was becoming too much of an addiction.

Holding her hand, he directed her back towards the steps carved into the cliff-face. Began to climb. 'Come on, I've never been

to a three-year-old's birthday party before. It
promises to be quite an experience.'

Feeling the warmth of his palm as he led
her up the steps—and hearing the genuine
warmth in his voice—Ruby struggled not
to read too much into the sense of achieve-
ment, and the tenderness she felt towards him.
Or the yearning for something she'd never
yearned for before, that had seized her ever
since she'd walked into Madeleine King's
home.

None of these emotions were significant.
Not really. Tomorrow she and Cal would be
going their separate ways. And everything
they'd shared over the last few days would be
forgotten.

CHAPTER FIFTEEN

'MADDY, could I have a word with you?' Cal asked, glad that his voice sounded even—and reasonably assured. It was late in the afternoon, the sun dropping low over the cliffs. He shaded his eyes against the glare, not quite sure what had propelled him out of the house when he'd spotted his sister busy tending her flower garden alone.

He hadn't actually intended to give in to Ruby's request. Had tried all through the day to dismiss their conversation and forget about it. Ruby didn't really know what she was talking about. He'd be mad to speak about something to Maddy that they'd both let go of years before.

But Ruby had got to him, even though he'd promised himself last night he wouldn't let that happen again. She'd triggered something inside him when he'd caught her talking with his sister in that hushed, confidential tone. And he'd lost his temper with her. And even though he'd managed to pull himself together, he couldn't seem to get his emotional equilibrium back.

And as the day had progressed, every damn stupid little detail had only unsettled him more. Watching his sister conduct the toddlers' tea party with calm unruffled efficiency and undisguised joy. Seeing the way Ruby placed the cupcakes she'd baked onto the tea table with a proud flourish. Holding Mia's compact little body on his lap while she blew out her birthday candles. He'd felt as if he were an observer, an outsider in his own family's celebration. As if there were something missing in his life, even though he knew there couldn't be.

But no matter how hard he'd tried, he hadn't been able to make the hollow feeling in the pit of his stomach go the hell away. And so he'd been forced to concede that maybe Ruby had a point.

He owed Maddy an apology. Not just for the way he'd acted towards her yesterday evening. But for the way he'd behaved for years—because it had always been easier to shut her out than to admit the truth. That he'd failed her terribly when they were children.

Maybe if he finally got all that off his chest, everything would go back to the way it was supposed to be.

'Sure.' Maddy stood up, brushing the mud off her jeans and tucking her hair behind her ear. With her gardening clothes on, and the bright grin on her face, she looked impossibly young and carefree, reminding him painfully of the boisterous girl who had eventually been beaten down by their parents' enmity. How come he had never seen it until today? That marrying Rye and having a family of her own had brought that bright lively child back? Made her become the person she was always meant to be?

'But can I say something first, Cal?' She took his hand in both of hers, lifted it to her cheek. 'Thank you for coming. And thanks for chipping in at the party. Mia had a wonderful time.' She laughed. 'It's meant so much to me having you here.'

Oh, hell.

He tensed, staring at the glitter of emotion in her eyes, not sure this had been such a great idea after all.

'I know we make you uncomfortable.' Her

voice sobered. 'I'm sorry for that. I hope now it'll be easier for you to come whenever you want. But I'm going to stop pressuring you about it. You only have to visit when you feel like it.'

She let his hand drop, a soft sigh escaping from her lips.

'You didn't pressure me, Mads,' he murmured, using the childhood nickname for the first time in years. 'And you didn't make me uncomfortable. I did that all by myself. There's something I should have told you. And I didn't.'

The beatific smile on her lips turned to one of curiosity. 'I don't understand?'

And so he told her. At first he couldn't look at her. So he stared out across the lawns towards the sea, the tumbling breakers matching the turmoil swirling under his ribcage as he forced himself to tell his sister the truth. The sordid details spoken in a tight monotone sounded all the more ugly, the more dirty, against the fresh salty scent of the sea air and the bold beautiful colours of Maddy's garden.

She listened quietly, asking only the odd question. Her smile had faltered, flattened once his gaze finally met hers. But the disgust, the reproach he had expected to see in her face never materialised. Instead all he saw was a steady acceptance.

As he finished one lone teardrop fell, which she brushed away hastily.

Rising on tiptoe, she wrapped her arms around his shoulders and kissed his cheek. 'You shouldn't have had to bear such a terrible burden all by yourself.'

'I shouldn't have kept it from you.' It all seemed so obvious now. Why had he never seen what Ruby had spotted after only a day? 'I wish I'd told you sooner.'

Maddy's lips curved into a sweet, sunny smile. 'So do I. But at least now you have.' She looped her arm through his, fell into step beside him as they walked back to the house. 'Tell me, did Ruby have anything to do with your decision to finally talk to me about it?'

He gave a stiff shrug, just the mention of Ruby's name sending his emotions spinning again.

She was the most infuriating, most impulsive, most reckless woman he'd ever encountered. So how did she manage to turn him inside out with lust? Make his head feel as if it were exploding with frustration every time she challenged him? And at the same time cut

right through the control that he relied upon
for his sanity?

'I'm not saying a word, on the grounds it
might incriminate me.'

Or push me over the edge into insanity.

Maddy sent him a wistful smile. 'Sometimes I think you're too clever for your own
good, Cal.'

He slung his arm over her slim frame, gave
her an easy hug as she pressed against his
side. 'I try to be,' he said. Although right at
the minute, he'd never felt more stupid.

He'd done what Ruby suggested, told
Maddy the truth at last, so why didn't it feel
like enough?

As he stepped into the living room with
Maddy at his side, he spotted Ruby chatting
with Rye in front of the big picture window.
She glanced round, and the light from the setting sun caught the red highlights in her hair.

Her eyes met his and Cal felt the foolish
bump under his breastbone and the way his
heart scrambled into his throat.

Blast, he hadn't sorted out a damn thing.

CHAPTER SIXTEEN

'MADDY and Rye and Mia are wonderful,' Ruby murmured, staring out of the Ferrari's windscreen. The drystone walls and lush greenery of the Cornish countryside whipped past, the dramatic landscape only making the turmoil of conflicting emotions more acute. 'Thanks for inviting me along. I had a great time.'

'You and Maddy became fast friends,' Cal commented. 'I noticed she invited you to come down in October.'

His voice was gruff, laconic, and she wondered if she detected a note of censure in the tone. Was he concerned that she might be foolish enough to take Maddy up on the offer?

'Yes, that was sweet of her. But I won't be able to make it,' she said, firmly. 'The business is mental in October because of all the Halloween and fireworks parties we cater for.'

However much she might want to, she wasn't going to visit Maddy again. She wasn't an imbecile. Suppose Cal turned up too with a new woman on his arm? Talk about awkward.

Although somehow it didn't feel like awkwardness or embarrassment making the leaden feeling in her stomach plummet to her toes when he remained silent.

'I see,' he said at last.

The ball of emotion in her throat grew. She swallowed it down, determined not to give in to the pointless weakness. What on earth had she expected? That he would suggest she come as his date?

That wasn't going to happen. Just because he'd made love to her last night as if he couldn't do without her. Just because she'd seen the astonishment on his face when Mia had given him a spontaneous hug after blowing out her candles. Just because she'd noticed that strangely unguarded look in his eye when he'd walked into the house with Maddy an hour ago. Just because he appeared to have spoken to his sister as she had suggested.

It did not mean a single thing.

Sex was what they did best. So of course the physical connection would be heightened on their last night together. She'd found a kindred spirit in Maddy—and she'd hit it off with Rye and Mia too—so why wouldn't she be a little emotional knowing she would never see them again?

This had nothing to do with Cal. Or the idiotic hope that had blossomed inside her during the children's party, and afterwards while they'd said goodbye to Maddy and her family, that there might be a chance they could continue their affair.

No way was she holding her breath, waiting for him to suggest they see each other again. She didn't wait for guys to ask her out. She did the asking if she wanted. And she didn't. All this weekend had proved was that she'd allowed herself to become addicted to Callum Westmore. His skill and stamina in bed were phenomenal so that was no big surprise. He was going to be a hard act to follow.

No pun intended.

A weak smile curved her lips as she heard him shift down to take another tight bend.

Okay, maybe she'd also discovered a depth to him, an emotional integrity she certainly hadn't expected. And a surprising vulnerability behind that controlled exterior. But that didn't make them any more compatible than they had been two days ago... Cal wasn't looking for love, or commitment. He didn't trust it. And she couldn't change that.

'Do you mind if I have a nap?' she asked, suddenly desperate for the oblivion of sleep. She wanted the treacherous thoughts to stop jumping around in her head. The pointless yearning to stop tugging at her heart.

'Sure, go ahead.'

She heard the frown in his voice, but couldn't look at him.

Letting her mind drift off, she prayed that she'd be able to stay in a coma for the rest of the six-hour drive. Foolish tears stung her eyes and she gulped them down ruthlessly.

Get real, Ruby Delisantro. Remember, you don't want what Maddy and Rye have. Not yet. You're not ready. And you'd certainly never find it with a man like Callum Westmore.

But as her mind eventually clicked off, and she fell into an exhausted sleep, she couldn't seem to recall all the very good reasons why.

Cal merged the car into the traffic on the M5 and pressed his foot to the floor. He wanted to get this damn drive over with as fast as possible. If Ruby stayed asleep long enough, he might have some hope of getting them both back to London and bidding her goodbye before he did something really stupid.

He and Ruby did not have a future together. Even in the short term. So this was where their affair had to end.

Sure Ruby had made him see things he should have seen years ago. And maybe their relationship had grown more intense than he would usually have allowed. He admired her zeal and her tenacity, her capable mind and her refusal to back down. But none of that was important. Not in the long run. Because he didn't want permanent in his life. And Ruby was the sort of woman who, when she finally chose to commit, would do it without holding back. She had a big heart beneath that super-sexy exterior—she would want love as well as passion and that was something he didn't have it in him to give her.

This weekend, his whole life had shifted on its axis. He'd been forced to face the truth about himself and his past and the experience had left him emotionally raw in a way he wasn't used to. No wonder he was behaving irrationally.

He caught a whiff of the sultry vanilla scent that permeated the car. Something about this woman had the ability to drive him crazy—she shouldn't have a hold on him, and yet somehow she did.

The only way to stop this madness was to let her go. But as the powerful sports car ate up the miles, bringing them closer and closer to London, he could literally feel his resolve ebbing away, like water from a leaky dam... until the only barrier that was left was pride. He couldn't ask Ruby to continue their affair, because it would give her too much power over him. And she had far too much already.

But if she asked him first, or at least gave him an indication that she wanted him as much as he wanted her. Then he'd be able to set the terms. And risk taking her back into his bed, for a little while longer.

'How about I carry the bag up for you?' Cal said as he lifted Ruby's leather holdall out of the car and slammed the boot.

Ruby's heartbeat skittered, but then she spotted the car keys dangling from his finger. He was offering to carry her bag. He wasn't offering anything else.

'No need, I've got it from here.' She grasped

the handle, careful not to let her fingers touch his, and took the bag. Sweeping her hair back from her face, she sent him what she hoped was a detached smile. Not easy with her heart battering her chest. 'It's been fun, Cal. But I'm shattered.'

She turned away, the sting of tears perilously close. She'd have to kill herself if he saw her cry, so she picked up the pace. The sooner she was on her own, the better, then she could snap out of this damn silly mood she seemed to be in.

'Hang on. Don't I even rate a goodbye kiss?' he shouted after her. The statement sounded stiff, gruff, with none of his usual relaxed charm. Her heart careered painfully into her chest wall and the blockage in her throat grew.

She stopped and spun round. The sight of his long, muscular body spotlit by the street light as he leaned against the polished wing of the sports car made the dragging feeling in her belly twist into a knot.

'I'll pass, thanks.' The tight smile on her lips felt as if it had been carved in stone. She touched her fingertips to her cheek. 'I don't want to risk another whisker burn.'

She stood transfixed by the brittle green

glitter in his eyes as he watched her for what seemed like an eternity. Her throat hurt with the struggle to stem the tears, her knuckles whitening on the handle of the bag as she tried to hold back the foolish spurt of hope that had refused to die throughout the endless journey home—during most of which she'd pretended to be fast asleep.

The distant sound of a siren wailed, cutting through the tension like a blade. He shrugged. 'Fair enough.' Pushing away from the car, he flipped the keys up and caught them in his palm. Then sent her a mocking salute. 'See you round, Ruby.'

Seconds later he had got into the car, revved the engine and roared away from the kerb.

Ruby's heart imploded as her vision blurred and her throat closed over the whispered words. 'Not if I see you first, Callum.'

CHAPTER SEVENTEEN

'Ow!' Ruby yelped, the tray of newly baked cupcake sponges clattering onto the work surface.

'Are you okay?' Ella rushed across from the mixer.

Ruby nodded as she sucked her palm where the skin burned, holding back the urge to scream. But only just.

It had been two weeks now since Callum Westmore had driven out of her life. But this morning she'd finally had to face the truth, as she'd dragged herself out of bed after another night spent struggling to sleep, while the wild unbidden images tossed around in her brain and her body ached as if it had been battered with a baseball bat.

She'd developed some sort of obsession for her wild weekend fling.

A man she'd known for all of three days.

A man who was totally wrong for her but her mind and body had somehow decided was totally right.

She couldn't be in love with him, because that wouldn't make any sense. She'd been in love before and it didn't feel anything like this. Love was easy, effortless, painless, pleasant. One of life's little joys. This strange yearning she had to see Callum again wasn't painless or pleasant or joyful. It hurt. And she hadn't been able to let go of it however hard she'd tried. Plus, she'd never, ever been the one to fall first, because that would be incredibly stupid. And she'd never been a stupid woman.

But if it wasn't love, what was it? And why couldn't she seem to get over it?

Ella cradled her hand and stared at the livid red line. 'Ouch. That's the third time you've scalded yourself this week.'

'I know,' Ruby muttered as she allowed her friend to lead her to the sink.

The cold water splashed over the raw skin, dousing the fiery pain in her palm. But doing nothing to alleviate the aching, ever-present pain in her chest.

Her mother had once told her the story of how she'd fallen in love with her father. How it had literally been love at first sight. When they'd both been children in Italy together.

Ruby had thought the story wildly romantic as a girl. And ever so slightly ridiculous as a teenager. And after her mother had died, and her family had fallen to pieces, she'd begun to question whether it was even true. How could her mother have loved her father and then slept with another man?

But she'd been thinking about her mother's fanciful story more and more in the last two weeks. Ever since Callum and she had parted. And right now the thought that it might be true, that you really could fall in love with someone in the space of a minute—or even a few days—filled her with fear. She didn't want to be beholden to someone like that. Fully and completely and without prejudice and for ever. She'd breezily told Callum in Cornwall that love mattered. That it was much more than lust. But she wasn't feeling quite so blasé about it any more. What if love snuck up on you when you weren't looking? And you couldn't say no to it?

She shook the thought away. She was being silly. Ridiculous. The trip to Maddy's had just made her realise how much she missed having a family. She'd spent years denying the need inside her for that kind of lasting, loving connection because she'd always been scared that it could blow up in her face, as it had before. Maddy and Rye had made her realise that the risk could be worth it. And then she'd taken her admiration for the couple, her yearning for the simple contentment of their life together, and somehow fixated on Cal.

Which was perfectly understandable.

Her live-wire attraction to him right from the first moment she'd set eyes on him. The way she'd basked in his approval. The electric zing of excitement whenever she'd been in his company and that compelling feeling of connection as she'd discovered a depth to his character she'd never expected. All those qualities had made him the perfect candidate for her newfound desire to start a family.

And also perfectly ridiculous.

Because Callum Westmore wasn't interested in family or love or happily ever after. He'd said as much, and people didn't lie about that stuff. And given what his father had put him through, it was no big surprise he found it impossible to trust anyone.

The only problem was, even knowing that, she couldn't stop thinking about him. She'd go from being euphoric at the mere thought of him, to crushingly sad at the thought that she'd never see him again. In the process she'd lost the ability to work, or sleep, or function like a normal person. And her business was suffering as a result.

She couldn't contact Callum. What would she say? That she wanted to extend their weekend fling? That she wanted to have a relationship with him? He'd made it perfectly plain he wasn't in the market for anything like that. And how would she explain the way she felt about him, when she couldn't even explain it to herself?

She had to snap out of it. That much was obvious.

'Does this have something to do with that guy?' Ella said softly as she soothed antiseptic gel over the burn. 'Callum Whatshisname.'

'How did you guess?' Ruby sighed.

She'd tried not to let her insanity show. Had resisted confiding in Ella because it would only make the confusion more real, more tangible. And up until this morning she'd clung to the vague hope that the train wreck her life had become might be nothing more than a bad case of great sex withdrawal.

It was way past time to stop kidding herself.

Maybe she'd never be able to forget Callum completely. Their sexual connection had been pretty intense. But that didn't mean she could carry on obsessing about him. She had a business to run, for pity's sake. And a perfectly nice, happy and fulfilling social life she wanted to get back to without this aching feeling of emptiness and futility dogging her every move.

'So he's The One?' Ella said, her voice hushed in awe.

'He most certainly is not The One,' Ruby said sharply. A bit too sharply. 'He's just the one who got away.'

So far it had only been a fortnight, she told herself staunchly. This silly yearning to spend time with Callum, to explore every single facet of his character, would fade eventually. It had to.

Picking up the tray of cupcake sponges, she began transferring them to the icing sheet. She needed to immerse herself in work, and stop thinking about him constantly. That would be an excellent start.

'Do you want to talk about it?' Ella said, her voice subdued.

She did want to talk about it. She wanted to talk about every minuscule detail of their time together. Even the arguments. But that was the delusional person talking. The delusional person she'd decided to ignore. 'Not particularly,' she said.

The melodic ding of the doorbell made one of the cupcakes jerk out of her hand. The little spurt of excitement was instantly quashed. Cal wasn't going to call on her, and she didn't want him to. She was having enough trouble forgetting Mr Unforgettable without him turning up on her doorstep and making matters worse.

'I'll get it,' Ella said, giving Ruby's back a gentle rub before heading for the front reception area.

Minutes later, her friend came dashing back, brandishing a letter. 'You have registered post, Rube. And it's from him.'

'What?' She blinked. 'How do you know that?'

Ella thrust the letter into her hand. 'There's a return address.'

Holding the thin white envelope with the registered mail sticker on it, Ruby's hands trembled as she read the Lincoln's Inn address, written in a swirling serif font with Callum Westmore, QC emblazoned at the top.

'Open it, then.' Her friend gave her a nudge.

Ruby sliced open the envelope with one of the kitchen carving knives. The thick white paper inside was stamped with the same letterhead. As she unfolded it another piece of paper fluttered onto the work surface. She stared at it. A cheque made out to her for a thousand pounds.

Why on earth…?

Then her gaze strayed back to the note, her heart pounding so hard now she could barely breathe as she read the three concise sentences written in a bold black scrawl.

Ruby,
We had fun a couple of weeks ago. Let's have more.
Contact me.
Cal

'What's all that money for?' Ella piped up beside her as Ruby sucked in a shaky breath.

Screwing up the note, she threw it in the dustbin, hitting the wicker dead on and making it rattle. Even though she knew she was overreacting, she couldn't seem to stop herself. Her heart felt as if it were being ripped from her chest.

For one blissful moment, she'd believed something wonderful was going to happen. And she wasn't even sure what that wonderful thing was. Just that Cal had contacted her, he wanted to see her again. And that meant anything was possible.

But then his curt, cursory words had registered, and the full impact of the insulting payment. And everything had crashed down into the pit of despair opening up like a chasm inside her.

It was worse. Much worse than she had imagined. She'd thought that although he didn't care for her enough to even consider a relationship, that at least they had parted as friends. That this silly yearning hadn't been completely one-sided. But the note showed she had never been more than an available body. A willing available body. No doubt like all the other women he'd dated and then discarded.

Fury rose up to quell the vicious, inexplicable pain. She shoved the cheque in the pocket of her apron, whisked her car keys

off the hook by the ovens and charged out of
the door.

'The money is for Callum Westmore's funeral expenses.'

CHAPTER EIGHTEEN

Ruby drove to his flat first. Stabbed on the intercom for ten minutes, allowing the simmering rage to dry up all of her tears. She'd shed them later, after she'd confronted him. Seeing him again would be hard, but not as hard as letting him rob her of the last of her pride and self-respect.

No man got to waltz into her life, waltz back out again, turn her into a basket case and then kick her while she was down.

She'd invented the man she thought he was. The sensitive, traumatised boy who'd become a man of such rigid control that he'd closed himself off from even the possibility of love.

That had all been an illusion brought about by sex and emotion and a lack of sleep—and her own stupidity. Callum Westmore wasn't the troubled, turbulent man she'd discovered over that long-lost summer weekend.

She'd always been impulsive, passionate, and reckless—and in Callum she'd met a man who knew how to exploit that, by giving her an out-of-body experience in bed. Probably not unlike the man who had once made her mother forget the man she loved for one night of thoughtless passion.

She closed her fist over the cheque, stabbed the button again, ready to throw the offending scrap of paper in his face when he opened the door.

But, he didn't.

Damn, he wasn't in.

The letterhead on his note had included an address in Lincoln's Inn, one of the prestigious Inns of Court in central London. Forcing her mind to engage, she flagged down a cab.

He must have his chambers there, and on a Friday morning he was probably working. She was in no condition to drive—and she needed to stay in one piece until she confronted Cal and told him where he could stick his insulting offer.

When she arrived at the hallowed oasis of historic buildings and manicured garden squares tucked behind the Strand, the imposing eighteenth-century façade of red stone and leaded glass only fuelled her temper. Was it any surprise that Cal would never be able to appreciate what she had to offer? They came from two different worlds—he righted wrongs for a living and she baked cupcakes. The connection she'd felt so strongly in Cornwall seemed a million miles away in the lofty legal environs where Callum Westmore QC had forged a meteoric legal career.

She had led with her emotions instead of her intellect and she supposed she deserved to be punished for that, but she didn't intend to be the only one suffering.

It took her ten minutes more to find the building that housed the chambers referred to in Callum's letter. Polished oak panelling and centuries-old stone masonry made the place reek of gravity and importance—doing nothing to quell the inadequacy twisting in Ruby's stomach. Entering a large room full of men in suits, Ruby was directed to a fresh-faced young man sitting at a desk piled high with files.

'I need to see Callum Westmore,' she blurted out, grateful that her pitch was only slightly shrill.

The man's gaze flicked down her figure and she realised she still had her flour-stained pinny on. 'You'll have to make an appointment.'

She stifled the blush. 'Is he here?'

'He's in court.' The man glanced at his watch. 'And he has another case at twelve. So he won't be able to see you today.'

'Could you please just contact him and say Ruby Delisantro is waiting? It's personal.'

Hysteria bubbled under her breastbone at the thought that she couldn't contact him herself. How could he have come to mean so much when his phone number wasn't even programmed into her mobile? She clamped down on the urge to run, suddenly unsure and confused.

What was she even doing here? What did she hope to achieve? Was this really just some pathetic excuse to see him one more time? What had become of the smart, confident, self-assured woman she'd always believed herself to be?

The young man kept a watchful eye on her as he made the call in hushed tones. He put down the phone. 'If you'd like to wait over there,' he said coolly, indicating two leather armchairs placed at the corner of the office, 'he'll be here shortly.'

The rapid ticks of her heartbeat pummelled

her ribs as she stood next to the chairs and watched the heavy oak entrance door—only too aware of the many pairs of eyes she could feel boring into her back. Clearly Lincoln's Inn wasn't often graced with irate pastry chefs on the verge of a nervous breakdown.

Cal strode in moments later. A flowing black robe draped over his broad shoulders and billowed out behind him, accentuating his tall frame and dark, compelling features. The green gaze locked on hers. 'Ruby?'

Her breath caught and for a second that seemed to last a lifetime she stood rooted to the spot.

His lips curved into a sensual smile as he crossed the carpeted lobby area towards her. 'It's good to see you,' he said, the casual pleasantry given an erotic overtone by the rough murmur of his voice.

Ruby drew in a staggered breath.

How could the memory of those firm lips on hers, those long, talented fingers stroking heated flesh, still be so vivid? How come she could still recall the exact shape of his chin, the flecks of moss green in the emerald hue of his irises, the woodsy scent of his shampoo? How could the rough, steady tone of his voice still heat her insides like hot chocolate? She thrust her hand into the apron pocket before she gave in to the desire to plunge her fingers into his hair—and touched the cheque. Misery and fury tangled in her belly, right alongside the desire and the wistful tug of longing.

Closing her fist over the scrap of paper, she threw it at him. 'I came to give you this.'

One dark brow winged up. Shifting his gaze to the floor, he bent to pick up the crumpled cheque. 'Why?'

'Because I'm not your whore, that's why,' she snapped, the words remarkably calm and clear considering her throat had thickened so much it was blocking off her oxygen supply.

The other brow arched up his forehead. 'When did I ever say you were?'

'The money. What was it for? Services rendered?'

Instead of looking guilty or even embarrassed, his brows flattened. Strolling towards her, he gripped her upper arm. 'Let's take this upstairs,' he said wryly. 'Before my reputation is completely ruined.'

As he guided her through the main door she heard the hushed whispers, detected the strained silence as the young man gaped at her and all the other clerks stared with avid curiosity. But she was past caring as Cal propelled her towards a wide sweeping staircase. She wrestled her arm out of his grasp, swung round to face him.

'*Your* reputation?' She shoved him with her palm. 'What about *my* reputation? You paid me money for sleeping with you. Or was it a bribe to get me to sleep with you again?'

His exasperated curse echoed in the stony silence. 'Why is nothing ever easy with you?' Before she could guess his intent, he caught her round the waist, bent over and hefted her over his shoulder.

'Stop it, put me down.' She kicked, struggled.

He held her legs down, ignoring her protests as he marched up the stairs. 'Be quiet, Ruby,' he said coolly. 'And stop punching me, or I'm going to take great pleasure in paddling your very nice behind.'

Striding down a long, panelled hallway, he burst into one of the rooms at the end and dumped her unceremoniously into a leather armchair.

She grasped the armrests, ready to leap out of it, but his hands came down on hers, caging her in.

'The money was for the damage to your car,' he said, his voice low with annoyance.

'My…? What?' She dropped back into the seat, the fighting spirit draining out of her.

'Your car.' He stood up, that searing green gaze slicing right through her indignation. 'We agreed I would pay for the damage.'

'But it only cost two hundred,' she murmured, choking on the denial as the brutal blush blazed up her neck and set her scalp on fire. What had she done? 'A thousand pounds is too much.'

'So give me a damn refund.'

He paced across the room, thrusting his fingers into his hair. Standing with his legs akimbo, he stared out of the large, mullioned window into the courtyard below. 'Do you have any idea how much legal clerks love to gossip?' he murmured. 'You've just given them enough fodder to keep us feeding the rumour mill for a month.'

Shame filled her at what she'd shouted at him. 'I'll explain. To the people downstairs.'

She stood, her legs trembling, more unsettled and unsure of herself than ever. Why had she jumped to all the wrong conclusions? What had possessed her to come storming in here, accusing him?

He turned. 'Forget it,' he said. 'It's my fault

as much as yours. I should have explained in my note.'

But it wasn't his fault. It was hers. And now she knew why. Because she'd done the unthinkable. The one thing she wanted to believe wasn't possible. This wasn't an addiction. It wasn't a fixation. He meant much more than that to her. And she'd wanted to mean more than that to him.

She crossed to the door.

'Where are you going?' The words made the skin on her neck prickle.

'I'm leaving.'

'No, you're not.' She heard his footsteps, her hand stilling on the door handle as a new heat rose inside her to join the searing pain of humiliation and confusion.

'Don't go.' Warm hands settled on her waist, tugging her back against his chest. He wrapped his arms around her. 'I've missed you, Ruby,' he murmured, hot breath brushing across her nape. 'Even though you're the most troublesome woman I've ever met.'

She shuddered, the shock of reaction, the desperate need in her heart for him to mean it—to really mean it—making her soften into him.

'Seeing as you've come all this way,' he

added, pressing tantalising kisses to the sensitive skin beneath her ear, 'we might as well make the most of the opportunity.'

'Don't.' She placed her hands over his, tried to break his hold, but all the strength had left her. 'I didn't come for this.'

'Didn't you?' His teeth nipped at her ear lobe, sending another shudder through her system.

She moaned. The sound low and feral and full of the need she'd tried so hard to hide, to pretend didn't exist. 'I can't.' Her voice broke on the words, doing nothing to disguise the lie. She wanted more. So much more. Was it possible he might want more too?

'Yes, you can,' he whispered. 'You want this as much as I do.'

She felt the low liquid pull in her belly. Her nipples squeezed into hard, rigid peaks as his hands rose up her torso. The coarse canvas of the apron stimulated the tender flesh of her breasts as he massaged through the layers of clothing.

She twisted in his arms, gripped his face in unsteady hands. She couldn't wait, couldn't give herself time to think. This wasn't just about sex. It couldn't be.

'Make love to me,' she whispered, feeling

the hope that she'd kept so carefully leashed blossom.

With one swipe he swept the leather-bound books off the desk. The heavy thuds as they hit the carpet echoed the pounding of her pulse as he lifted her onto the cold mahogany, and settled between her thighs.

She reached for his trousers, frantic to free him before sanity returned. He swore softly, the sound of rending silk sending her senses into overdrive as he ripped aside the final barrier.

The hard thrust lodged him deep, forcing her body to bow back, arch upwards. She groaned, sobbed, the penetration too full, too sudden. Gripping her hip, he delved between them, finding her clitoris. Exposing the swollen nub, he began to move, the strokes forcing him deeper still as he caressed her core. She powered over that brutal edge with shocking speed, the loss of control a maelstrom of emotion as she buried her head in his neck, clung to broad shoulders.

He shouted out his own release, still seated deep.

The rasps of their breathing sounded like the roar of cannon fire in the silent solemnity of his office. A shame far greater than any she could ever have imagined settled over her as the musty scent of sex and the discomfort of the still firm erection pulsed inside her.

Tears welled, slid down her cheeks as emotion crushed her chest and her fingers fisted in the short dark hair.

How could something that had seemed so pure, so perfect a second before, suddenly be so sordid? She sat even now on his desk, her skirt bunched around her waist, her legs wrapped around his hips. Nausea churned at the thought of how wrong she'd been.

Was this how her mother had felt, when she'd betrayed her father?

In her desperation to make Cal love her, she'd proved exactly the opposite. That sex was all they had ever really shared.

Blinking furiously, scrubbing the tears away with the heel of her hand before he spotted them, she pushed at his shoulder. 'I have to go.'

He lifted his head, caressed her hips, his pupils still black with arousal. 'I'm sorry. That didn't have a lot of finesse. Are you okay?'

'You need to move, so I can leave,' she said, unable to process what he was saying, hysteria racing back to the surface. The last thing she needed now was for him to be kind.

He pulled out of her and she scrambled up, all too aware of the sticky residue, the torn knickers as she clambered off the desk, brushed her skirt down, and swallowed the gulping sobs that threatened to spill out before she got away from him.

She made a beeline for the door, hearing the rasp of his zipper as he righted his own clothing. 'I'll see you around, Cal.'

'Wait just a damn minute.' He grabbed her as she reached the door, held on as she struggled.

She bit into her lip to stop it trembling. 'I need to go. I'm busy.'

'You're not going anywhere. We need to talk about what just happened. And where we go from here.'

'I'm fine. And we don't need to talk.' She'd rather die than talk about what they'd just done. 'Because it's over. There's nowhere to go from here.' He wanted to offer her crumbs when what she wanted was the banquet.

His eyes raked over her face. 'You're not fine. We do need to talk. And don't tell me we've got nowhere to go when we just proved this is a long way from being over.'

The phone on the desk buzzed.

'Damn it.' Keeping his grip on her with one hand, he grabbed the receiver with the other.

After a brief conversation, he slammed the phone back in its cradle. 'I've got to go. I have to be in court in ten minutes. But you're staying here. I'll tell Terry to send up some coffee, tea, whatever you want. This'll take fifteen minutes, twenty tops—it's only a request for an adjournment. When I get back we're *going* to have that talk.'

From the rigid expression on his face, she could tell arguing would be futile—and she didn't have the strength to do it anyway. 'I can't wait long.'

His brow creased. 'I mean it, Ruby. I expect you to be here when I get back.'

She nodded. 'I know.'

He would expect it, she thought as he left the room. Because he had spent his entire life making sure his emotions never derailed his common sense.

Unfortunately, she now knew she was nowhere near as smart.

She scribbled a quick note and placed it on the desk—the same desk where she had offered him her heart and he hadn't even realised—and then followed him out of the door, five minutes later.

CHAPTER NINETEEN

THE pulsating salsa beat energised Ruby's limbs as she let her friend Dan twirl her round in a practiced move, but couldn't penetrate the numbness that had settled over her ever since her crying jag that afternoon. The picture of Cal the last time she'd seen him came blasting back into her mind and she took a misstep. Her hip collided with Dan's and he stopped.

'Damn it Rube, you're ruining my rep as the best salsa-nista in Camden.'

'Sorry, Dan. I'm a bit off tonight,' she shouted above the clamour of dancing couples and loud music, the headache banding around her temple.

She shouldn't have come to Sol's. The place held too many memories. But when Dan had phoned, she'd had the stupid idea that getting out was a necessity.

Cal hadn't called, and she hadn't expected

him to after the note she'd left. But when the
phone had rung, and she'd felt the kick of anticipation, the pathetic shimmer of hope, she'd
convinced herself she had to take the first step
on her road to recovery. Tonight. And Dan
was the perfect first step. A close friend for
years, he was so outrageously camp at least
she wouldn't have to ward off any unwanted
advances tonight.

She had to stop wallowing in self-pity. So
she'd finally been caught out by love. And she
could see now it served her right. She'd dab-
bled with love for years, skirting the edges secure in the knowledge that she was too smart,
too self-aware to ever get caught in a trap she
couldn't get out of.

But all those times she had thought she was
in love before, it had never been true. She'd
kidded herself about the depth of her feelings because she'd enjoyed the romance, the
drama, the companionship. But now she understood. Real love was what Rye and Maddy
had. What her mother and father had once
had. It involved taking risks. It involved giving yourself unselfishly without the guarantee
it would be returned.

She had always been so angry with her
mother for telling her father about the affair,

about Nick's parentage. Why couldn't her mother have taken the secret to her grave with her and saved them all from the truth? But Ruby understood now how courageous her mother had been and how much she'd risked to keep the secret as long as she had. All through her marriage she'd shouldered the burden of guilt—a burden that had stopped her from being able to truly love her son— because she loved her husband so much. She hadn't been protecting herself with her silence, she'd been protecting him. But in the end, ravaged by the cancer, the burden had been too much to bear.

You had to earn love, and Ruby never had, because she'd never risked a thing.

How ironic that Cal should have been the one to figure out the truth, when he'd questioned her commitment to creating a family of her own that day on the beach.

And wasn't it just her tough luck that when she decided to risk everything and fall in love for real, it would be with a man who would never be willing to return the gift?

'I'd say you're more than a *bit* off, girl-friend,' Dan added forcefully. Taking her hand, he led her away from the dance floor. 'Sit down.' He held out the chair at their table.

She slumped into it. Her body numb, her mind not much better.

'What's wrong anyway?' Dan said, his eyes shadowed with concern. 'You look like death warmed up tonight.'

'Nothing's wrong. I'm just a bit—'

'Hey, isn't he the gorgeous stud you were here with a couple of weeks back?' Dan lifted a hand to wave at someone over her shoulder.

She grabbed his wrist, yanked his hand down. Too late. Horror and a sick kind of hope assailed her as she glanced over her shoulder and saw Cal walking through the crowd towards them.

Panic skittered up her spine. Not here, not now. She wasn't ready for this.

'I have to go.' Ignoring Dan's stunned protest, she grabbed her bag and ran.

Refusing to look back, she dodged through the crowds. Stepping onto the secluded balcony at the back of the club, she'd got less than three paces before she realised her mistake. There was no way out.

Footsteps echoed on the decking and sounded deafening even above the hum of music and Friday-night revelry. She held her bag to her midriff. Scared to turn round.

'You're not going anywhere, Ruby. So we might as well have that talk now.'

The sound of his voice, rough and low, forced her to face him. He stood only feet away. Reaching into the pocket of his jeans, he pulled out the note she'd left him before fleeing his office that afternoon. 'Perhaps you'd like to start by explaining what this means?'

She shivered despite the warmth of the summer evening. She mustn't crack. Not now. The only thing she had now was pride. 'It means exactly what it says.'

He flicked it open, read it out loud. '"There's nothing to talk about, Cal. We had fun, but now it's over. Don't contact me again."'

She tensed, prayed he wouldn't come any closer. To see the tremor in her hands, the bloodless knuckles as she clung to her bag. 'I think that pretty much sums it up.'

He took a step forward. She scrambled back.

'You call what happened in my chambers this afternoon *fun*?'

Her heart lurched. Kicked hard in her chest. She bit hard into her lip to stop the quiver.

Gave him a stiff nod as tears formed in her eyes.

'I'd say it was a lot more than that,' he added, taking another step. 'Wouldn't you?'

Her back hit the balcony rail. She shook her head, choked back a sob. Why was he doing this?

But as the light reflecting off the canal hit his face she didn't see challenge, or superiority. She saw confusion.

Reaching up, he cupped her cheek. She jerked her head back. 'Don't. Please don't touch me.'

'Why don't you want me to touch you?'

'I can't,' she murmured, staring down at her clasped hands. 'I can't do this any more.'

He thrust his hands into his pockets, shook his head. 'Why not?'

She shook her head furiously, the tears falling freely now. Of course, his logical, dispassionate nature would want to solve the problem. But she couldn't tell him. And have the last of her defences shattered.

'For God's sake, Ruby. You're crying!' He sounded horrified. 'What is it?' He took her chin in his fingers, lifted her face. 'You have to tell me so we can sort it out.'

'*We* can't sort it out. I have to sort it out on my own.'

'Why?'

She gulped down a sob and let go. 'Because I've fallen in love with you. And I know you can't love me back.'

The words dropped out into silence and she felt him go still. His hand dropped from her face. And her heart shattered all over again.

He swore under his breath.

She forced her chin up, brushed aside the errant tears that had escaped. 'It's all right, Cal. You don't have to say anything.'

The sea-green gaze searched her face. 'What makes you think you love me?' he asked, sounding stunned.

Pride kicked in at last, her spine straightening as she forced herself to smile. She patted his cheek, felt the familiar rasp of stubble. She'd said too much. Far too much. She needed to get out of here now. So she could go home and lick her wounds in private with at least a little of her dignity intact.

'Don't look so worried, Big Guy,' she said jauntily, giving an award-worthy performance. 'You're not the first. And you certainly won't be the last.'

But as she walked past him he grasped her

wrist. 'Ruby, don't go like this.' He hesitated, and for the first time since she'd met him she realised he was lost for words. 'I didn't mean to… Can we please talk about this?'

She forced a smile to her lips, but couldn't make herself meet his eyes. 'Don't be silly. It's not that big a deal.' She tugged her hand out of his grasp. 'I'll get over it. I always do.'

She heard his whispered curse above the sound of the salsa drums as she walked away, pathetically grateful that the tears cascading down her cheeks were masked by the moonlight.

CHAPTER TWENTY

CAL rapped his fountain pen against the desk as the tightly spaced type of the witness statement he was supposed to be reading bounced in front of his eyes. The hammer clicks of the pen sounded like machine-gun fire, and weren't making it any easier for him to concentrate. But he couldn't seem to keep still.

'Would you like me to contact Brady about the Carvelli witness?'

He glanced up at his clerk Terry's careful question. 'What?'

'The Carvelli witness.' Terry nodded towards the document in his hand. 'The one whose statement you've been reading for the last twenty minutes,' he prompted.

Cal stared blankly for several seconds, trying to will his mind to engage. 'No,' he said at last, when it resolutely refused to obey his command.

He put the papers down on his desk, caught his reflection in the varnished mahogany surface and sucked in a breath.

Sights, sounds and sensations flooded through his system—as they'd been doing far too frequently in the past week.

Ruby's full breasts heaving against the confining apron, her soft sobs echoing in his ear, her body clasped tight around his as he came—all wrapped in the scent of vanilla sponge cake, icing sugar and sex. Ruby's eyes meeting his, rising to any challenge.

'Let's do this tomorrow, Terry.' He pulled at the collar of his shirt, which felt as if it were strangling him.

Terry looked at him a moment, clearly torn. 'But the trial starts tomorrow and we haven't—'

'I know, I'll handle it.'

Terry nodded slowly, as if he were trying to placate a wild beast, then gathered up his papers and left. As soon as the door clicked shut behind him Cal hurled the pen across the room and watched it ricochet against the oak panelling.

'*Fun!*' The single word echoed off walls lined with leather-bound books. 'What the hell was fun about it, Ruby?'

Fantastic. Now he was talking to himself too.

Having spent a week, make that three weeks, ever since he'd returned from Cornwall in fact, thinking about one woman and one woman only, he'd discovered that he no longer had the ability to think about anything else. His focus, his concentration, his neat, tidy, well-ordered life had been blown to smithereens by a nuclear warhead known as Ruby Delisantro. And she'd had the audacity to call it *fun*.

What they had shared had never been fun. Not really. Not for him. And certainly not for her if how she'd looked at him the last time he'd seen her was anything to go by—the sheen of tears turning the chocolate brown of her eyes a rich caramel.

So why had she put it in her note? He winced. Maybe because he'd said the same thing in his.

Pushing back from the desk, he stood up and loosened his tie. Undoing the top two buttons of his shirt, he walked over to the chambers window and stared out at the lawn below where a couple of clerks were eating their lunch.

Those idiotic notes were just a couple of the

many mysteries about their relationship that he had been unable to solve. Nothing about their time together made any sense at all. He thrust his hand into his hair, furrowed it into rows.

Why had the sexual chemistry between them been so electric, for example, even though she'd never been his type? Why had she been able to get to him in ways no other woman ever had before? How had she been able to undermine his stability, his sense of certainty and make him question every single thing he'd ever taken for granted in his life in the space of a weekend? And why hadn't her declaration of love panicked him nearly as much as her assurance straight afterwards that she would get over it and him, with no trouble at all?

He cursed, flattened his forearm on the warm glass and rested his forehead against it.

He'd spent a whole week determined not to go after her again. Not to succumb to the bone-deep desire to promise her anything she wanted to get her back.

He didn't make promises, because he had always been terrified he wouldn't be able to keep them. But it was becoming blatantly obvious that staying away wasn't an option any more. Because the need to see her again was driving him completely nuts. And not just because he wanted to hold her again, to touch her, to explore her body and exploit the sexual attraction between them. No, he thought wryly. Wanting to see her for sex would have been far too simple, too straightforward.

And nothing about Ruby had ever been simple.

He didn't just want to see her for sex, even though he'd tried to make himself believe it when he'd written that ridiculous note, and then thrust inside her with about as much finesse as a battering ram when she'd come to his chambers.

He straightened, blew out a breath.

The truth was, he wanted so much more than sex from Ruby. He wanted to spend time with her. He wanted to talk to her. He wanted to inhale that spicy vanilla scent while discovering everything about her. Her favourite colour, her favourite book, her favourite film. What sort of music she listened to, even who she voted for—although he expected that discussion to cause more than a few arguments. He wanted to know what her best subjects were at school. The first thing she'd learned to bake. What her dreams were for her business. How she'd got the tiny crescent-shaped scar he'd noticed on her right hip. He even wanted to see her damn baby pictures. He was curious about her past, her present and every tiny thing in her life that had made her the strong, defiant, capable and yet caring woman she had become.

He frowned, squinting into the sunshine. It was madness, romantic in a way he'd always despised, but he couldn't shake the conviction that had been forming ever since he'd watched her walk away while he'd stood frozen in shock on the terrace of her friend's bar.

The conviction that they were connected. That they had so much more to learn, to discover about each other. That they weren't finished, but had only just begun. And that for the first time in his life he wanted to make a promise. To Ruby. And only Ruby.

'Damn it! What the hell are you waiting for, Westmore?'

A sudden sense of urgency propelled him across the room in four long strides. He grabbed up his wallet and his car keys and shoved them into the back pocket of his trousers. He'd wasted a whole damn week already, he thought as he dashed out of the door and strode down the corridor. He didn't care what Ruby said, or even what she wanted. She loved him. She'd said it herself. Which meant she was going to have to face the consequences.

No way in hell was she getting over him. Because he wasn't going to let her.

'Why don't we double the number of Chocolate Indulgence then and drop the Coffee Crumb altogether?' Ruby propped the specs back on her nose and marked the changes on her order sheet. 'Not a problem, Jamie. We aim to please.' She gave a forced laugh at the young executive's offer of a date, and turned him down, as she always did. But Jamie's relaxed flirting brought with it none of the pleasure it once had. Saying her goodbyes, she dropped the phone back in its cradle and flung her specs on the countertop.

'I can't believe how persistent that guy is,' Ella said from across the kitchen where she was busy cutting out cookie dough. 'You'd think he'd have taken the hint by now.'

Maybe he would have, Ruby thought, as she rubbed her neck where the muscles ached, if she hadn't once egged him on, enjoying their weekly flirting session as much as he did. Now all she wanted to do was curl up in a ball and never speak to another man again in her entire life. Because she didn't want any other man but Callum Westmore, and, unfortunately, he didn't want her. She sighed and grabbed her apron off the hook by the cooker.

'Time to snap out of it, Tess,' she muttered wearily.

'Who's Tess?' asked Ella.

Ruby glanced over her shoulder to encounter Ella's worried frown. 'Tess of the D'Urbervilles. My current role model. But luckily for you and everyone I know, I've just decreed that maudlin self-pity is far too unattractive.'

'It's only been a week, Rube. Give it time. You'll get over him.'

She sent Ella a weak smile. 'Good point.' Unfortunately she knew she would never get over Cal, because she had always been her mother's daughter, however much she had tried to deny it.

Once she fell in love for real, that was it for her.

'How about I make extras?' she said, rifling the cupboard for her ingredients. 'And we can have a Chocolate Indulgence Fest later with Prosecco and strawberries and watch that new crime series with the ultra hot tottie in.'

'That would be brilliant,' Ella said, perking up considerably and plastering on her usual cheery smile. Although that cheeriness had been a little forced of late.

The doorbell dinged.

'I'll get it,' Ella said, and left the kitchen.

Ruby crossed to the cold room to fetch six bars of luxury chocolate. She'd unburdened herself to Ella enough. Crying on her friend's shoulder was getting old. Maybe she would only be going through the motions for a while, but if she trained herself to look happy and carefree again, she might convince herself eventually.

'You can't come in! Haven't you upset her enough?'

Hearing Ella's pained shout, Ruby ducked out of the cold room.

And dropped the chocolate.

'What are you doing here?' she said, her voice soft as her heart rammed full pelt into her ribcage, so shocked at the sight of him, her knees began to shake.

'I told him he couldn't come in,' Ella said indignantly.

'I'm here to have that talk, whether you like

it or not,' Cal said firmly as he strode across the kitchen, his brows drawn down and his gorgeous face set in a determined frown.

He grasped her arm just as her knees buckled.

'You can't talk to her like—'

'It's okay, Ella,' she interrupted her friend's panicked plea, a little surprised by the steel in her voice as she locked her knees. 'Do you think you could leave us alone?'

'If you say so.' Ella slanted a furious look at Cal. 'But I'll be in the reception. If you need me,' she added, then left.

'You can let go of my arm now,' she said, oddly detached from the hysteria that was clutching at her chest.

His fingers released.

She'd let him say whatever he had to say, and then she'd let him go. 'So what was it you wanted to talk about?'

She probably deserved this. It was no doubt some sort of karmic revenge, for all those guys she'd played at being in love with and hadn't been.

'As if you don't already know.' He towered over her, the low fury in his voice matched by the swirl of temper in his eyes. 'You don't get to drop into my life, explode like an atomic bomb, and then just walk off and leave me to deal with the wreckage.'

Her back butted against the counter. She flattened her hands against his chest, but, instead of pushing him away, her fingers curled into the crisp cotton of his shirt.

'I don't know what you're talking about,' she said, panic and hope dog-fighting in her belly like dive bombers.

'Let me spell it out, then,' he snarled, furious now, his once-rigid control history. Gripping her waist, he lifted her onto the counter, then jerked her back towards him until her thighs were hugging his hips. 'You don't get to get over me, Ruby. Because I'm not going to get over you.'

'What are you trying to say?' she whispered. Hope winning, but only just.

He gave a deep sigh, dropped his head back and cursed at the ceiling.

She raised a hand to his cheek, brought his gaze back to hers. 'Don't you dare stop now, Cal. Or I may have to murder you.'

What she saw wasn't anger any more but soul-deep longing.

'I'm saying that this falling in love thing seems to be contagious,' he said, his lips tilting in a wry smile. 'And that perhaps we should give it a go together. See where it takes us.'

She stared at him, the hope swelling to impossible proportions as tears stung the backs of her eyes. 'Do not joke with me. Because it's not funny.'

He gave his head a rueful shake, wrapped his arms around her hips, drew her even closer, until her eyes were level with his.

'Ruby, how many women do you think I've said that to?' He touched his lips to hers, and she could have sworn she felt their hearts beating in unison. 'This is not the sort of thing I joke about. Ever.'

He cupped her cheek in his palm, the tenderness in his gaze as tangible as the heat. 'You drive me nuts.'

'I'm hoping that's a good thing,' she quipped, her flirt gene flickering to life as love bloomed inside her.

'And you've totally messed up my life. So much so that I don't ever want it to be that tidy again,' he said, his voice so rich with appreciation she felt her insides melt. His hand fell to her neck, caressed her collarbone. 'And you finally made me see the truth.'

'What truth?'

He huffed, looked away. 'I figured I was

like *him*. That I had the same weakness. The same inability to remain faithful. And that the best way to avoid breaking a promise would be never to make one.'

'But that's mad. You're nothing like your father,' she said forcefully, astonished that he could be quite that clueless about himself. 'How could you be? You're the most honourable man I know.'

He chuckled. 'If you say so.' He heaved a sigh. 'But that's not the point. It was never about him, it was about me. Being too much of a coward to trust anyone. To put myself out there and risk being hurt.'

She grinned, leaned into his palm. 'So all those things you said? About love being just a word?'

'Obviously complete rubbish. Thanks so much for pointing that out.'

She laughed, the bright happy sound underlaid by his rough chuckle.

'Are you sure you want to admit to that, Counsellor?' she purred, draping her arms over broad shoulders as the last of the anguish and confusion washed away on a tide of love and longing.

'I'll admit it under oath if you like,' he said,

sounding serious again as his hands ran down her back.

'That's very tempting.' She stretched, pressing the swollen tips of her breasts into his chest as she threaded her fingers into his silky hair. 'But I should warn you, I may use it against you at a later date.'

He chuckled. 'Feel free to use me all you want, Ms Delisantro.' Resting his hands on her hips, he pulled her against the proof of his love and desire. 'In fact, I'm counting on it.'

She rose up, pulled his mouth towards hers.

'Let's use each other,' she whispered, then placed a lavish kiss on his lips.

He angled his head, capturing her mouth to seal the deal.

And her heart did a victory roll before shooting off towards the cosmos.

EPILOGUE

'RUBY, thanks so much for the cupcake tower. It's fabulous. So fresh and funky. Everyone's talking about it.' Maddy beamed as she swayed gently from side to side in that unconscious way mothers did, with her newborn baby son sound asleep on her shoulder. 'I've had to give your details to four people already. It's like a work of art.'

'But hopefully a lot more edible.' Ruby grinned back at the woman who had become one of her favourite people. She laid her hand on little Daniel Callum King's back. She breathed in the sweet scent of talcum powder and milk. The soft bundle wriggled under her palm and her grin softened—the yearning across her chest tightening like a vice. *I want Cal's baby. I'm ready.* 'So, how's your little work of art doing?' she said, pushing the now almost constant longing as far away as she could.

Cal's hand squeezed her waist as he held her firmly against him. 'I think you may have a rock god in your future, Mads,' he said, has low rumble of laughter brushing against Ruby's hair. 'Given the amount of singing your son did in the church.'

'Not funny.' Maddy giggled. 'Rye reckons he may have deafened the vicar. And the poor old guy's hearing wasn't exactly pitch-perfect to begin with.'

'He's got a healthy set of lungs,' Cal said. 'All the better to top the charts with one of these days.'

'You wouldn't say that if you were the one getting up four times a night,' Maddy quipped.

'Well, you know what they say about making your bed and then having to lie in it…'

Ruby listened to brother and sister spar playfully with each other and took some comfort in the fact that their relationship had become so close and relaxed over the last few months. There was none of the distance that she'd seen between them last summer. She and Cal came down to Cornwall frequently now. Rye had started teaching him to surf, and he'd embraced his role as uncle with surprising enthusiasm. Although the first time the two of them had babysat Mia hadn't exactly been a roaring success—the little dynamo had managed to wind them both round her little finger, and when Maddy and Rye had returned from their dinner date at midnight, she and Cal still hadn't managed to get her into bed.

But Cal's words about his new nephew, even in jest, only made her yearning—and her confusion over it—more acute.

'Why don't I go and check on the tower, make sure it's not getting too depleted,' she said, interrupting the siblings' banter.

'You want me to give you a hand with that?' Cal asked, caressing her hip.

'No, I won't be long,' she said, suddenly eager to be alone and give herself time to think.

With the christening party in full swing, and the fifty or so guests happily enjoying the vintage champagne, Maddy's home-made canapés, and the glorious spring weather, it took Ruby quite a while to work her way through the crowd and escape to the solitude of the Trewan kitchen.

The decision to bake was probably a little manic but she decided to go with it. Hunting up the necessary ingredients from Maddy's well supplied pantry and putting an apron on to protect her posh frock, she began to rustle up a roast vegetable lasagne. Once everyone left, it would just be her and Cal, Rye, Maddy and the children and she doubted anyone had given much thought to supper.

Comfort food would be good for what ailed her.

She was being silly. Ridiculous. Letting the emotion of the day, and the sight of Cal holding his baby nephew that morning as they both made their vows as godparents, get to her in a big way.

This strange mixture of envy and hope and desperation was just a biological urge, one that had been nagging at her for a while and had gotten totally out of hand today. Watching Maddy's slim figure grow ripe with her child had been hard. But then, two weeks ago, when she and Cal had arrived at the Truro maternity hospital just after Danny's birth, the yearning had got a billion times worse. She'd had to bite her lip to stop herself from saying anything that night, when they'd been lying in each other arms and he'd been laughing about something Mia had said to him about her new baby brother.

Methodically scrubbing and chopping the vegetables, Ruby forced her mind to focus, so she could look at the situation rationally.

Cal and her had only been living together for seven months and while their relationship had brought her more joy than she could ever have imagined, it had also brought with it quite a few challenges. They were both headstrong, confident people who weren't shy about speaking their minds, and they didn't see eye-to-eye on everything. Far from it. Happily they were also both committed enough to each other to do whatever it took to find the middle ground. Heat bloomed at the memory of how their last argument had ended. One should certainly never underestimate the importance of great make-up sex when it came to navigating the minor bumps in a relationship.

The point was, she wanted to have Cal's children for the right reasons. She knew what an incredible father he would make. What incredible parents they would make together. They complemented each other, his logical, disciplined approach to life the perfect counterpoint to her passion and enthusiasm.

She sprinkled olive oil over the prepared

vegetables, seasoned them and popped the roasting tray into the oven.

But it was still way too soon.

That's what her head was shouting. Unfortunately, her heart and her biological clock were shouting something entirely different. And she was finding it harder and harder to reconcile the two.

Her heart lifted a little as she began to mix the pasta dough. Would it really be so terrible, just to mention it? In passing? After all, she knew Cal was unlikely to bring it up first. Like most guys it probably hadn't even occurred to him yet, because he didn't have a biological clock, ticking or otherwise.

She debated the pros and cons of placing the subject on the table, purely for the purposes of negotiation and discussion. Cal was highly unlikely to say yes straight off. She already knew that. He was a naturally methodical man. So she had to be prepared for Cal to say no, or not yet. And not let it upset her. She had to be prepared to be patient and pragmatic about his answer, before she posed the question. Or she could end up turning into even more of a ticking biological time bomb than she was already.

Unfortunately, patience had never been

Ruby's strong suit and pragmatism wasn't real big on her list of accomplishments either, unless it had to do with bulk ordering or filing Touch of Frosting's VAT returns in time. And she didn't think asking your partner if he would consider having a baby with you quite qualified.

'That smells incredible.'

Ruby yelped and dropped the sieve, sending a cloud of flour over herself and the counter.

'Cal, for goodness sake, are you trying to give me a heart attack?' she said as his arms circled her waist. The heat burned in her cheeks at the realisation that she'd been so deep in thought, she hadn't even heard him come in. Thank goodness he couldn't read minds, or she'd have more than the dusting of flour on her posh frock to worry about.

He laughed as he buried his face in her hair, inhaled deeply. 'You're a little jumpy aren't you?' He cuddled her, and her heart bumped against her ribcage.

God, she loved this man so much. What would she do if he said he never wanted to have children?

'And while I know I'm going to adore whatever it is you're cooking,' he added, his hands settling on her hips as he turned her to face him. 'Why are you hiding away in here? The party's not over yet. And it's not like you to miss out on the company—or the free champagne.'

'I'm not hiding.' She braced her hands on the countertop behind her, looked past him out the picture window. 'I just fancied a little peace and quiet, that's all. It's been a pretty hectic day.'

'You? Peace and quiet?' he scoffed. 'I don't think so.'

Tucking his forefinger under her chin, he brought her gaze to his. He looked amused and curious, and so gorgeous her heartbeat skidded into her throat.

'Now are you going to tell me what's been bothering you?' he asked mildly. 'Or am I going to have to wheedle it out of you?'

The heat blazed hotter in her cheeks. Had she really been that obvious? 'Nothing. Nothing's bothering me. I'm fine.'

'Forget it, Ruby,' he said. 'The gig's up. You might as well spill it now, or be prepared to be ravaged into submission later.'

She wanted to smile at his teasing. But she just couldn't. She swallowed. This was it. The moment of truth. And however ready or not ready they were to take this next step, she couldn't hold back the yearning to at least know where she stood a second longer.

'I've been thinking about children.' She cleared her throat, the sudden blockage coming from nowhere. 'About us. And children. And whether we want to have any. Or not.'

Instead of looking stunned, or worse, horrified, his smile barely faltered. 'I see.'

'So what do you say? Are you in favour of the idea?' She tried to be brusque, businesslike. Not easy with her heart now pummelling her larynx. 'You know, in principal, that is. We only have to make a decision in principal at this point. Obviously we don't have to start trying straight away. I'm only twenty-eight, we've got a few years yet before we have to worry about…' Her voice trailed off.

She was babbling. She sounded like a nincompoop.

'Well, say something,' she said, starting to get a little annoyed by the dimples deepening in his cheeks. 'Why are you smiling like that? It's not supposed to be…'

'It sounds like a wonderful idea,' he interrupted. His hands gripped her sides as he pressed her back against the countertop. 'How about we get started right now?'

She braced her arms against his chest, her

temper kicking in. 'This isn't a joke, Cal. I'm serious.'

'I know you are,' he said, the grin widening. 'So am I.'

'But…?' Her mouth dropped open. 'You are?'

That couldn't be right. She'd been agonising over asking him for weeks now, months even. He never made a decision without judging every piece of advice, weighing each iota of relevant information carefully. It had taken him a week to choose a new TV. It was one of the things she loved about him. He couldn't possibly have made up his mind in three seconds flat.

'But aren't you going to think about it first?' she murmured, still reeling.

He shrugged, his palms warm on her back. 'What's there to think about? You'd make an amazing mother. And I'm sure I can manage to make a halfway decent Dad if I set my mind to it. We'll probably make mistakes, all parents do. But that's all part of the adventure.'

'But, I…' She couldn't speak. Excitement and love and total shock combining to make her tongue numb.

'Ruby, I love you. I adore just being around

you. The last seven months have been the best of my life. Even though you still can't follow instructions worth a damn,' he teased. 'When I come home at night and you're there, I have to kick myself, because I can't believe how lucky I am to have you. We make a great pair. I'd never have considered having children with anyone else. But with you, it makes sense.'

Tears welled in her eyes. They made sense. That was it. And here she'd been tying herself in knots about the question, when the answer had always been there, right in front of her.

He brushed the tear away with his thumb. 'I'm hoping those are happy tears.'

She gave his arm a little punch, laughed. 'You know they are.'

'Good, because there is one small hitch in your plan.'

'What's that?'

'As you know I'm a logical, boringly conventional guy. I like to do things in their proper order. And what we have here is definitely a cart-before-horse situation.'

Ruby blinked and sniffed. 'What?' He'd totally lost her again, but she was willing to give him the chance to explain, because the wave of euphoria inside her was kind of hard to contain.

'Before we have a baby, or babies. I want my ring on your finger. And your signature on a marriage certificate.'

'You do?' She hadn't actually thought she could be any happier, but now she was.

'I definitely do,' he said, gathering her close.

He slanted a kiss across her lips.

As always the passion ignited between them instantly. But before she could get completely carried away, Ruby struggled back and held him at arm's length.

'Not so fast, Westmore. If that's your idea of a proposal, it's pathetic.'

He chuckled, hauling her up to seat her on the countertop and step between her thighs. 'I guess I'm going to have to work on it,' he murmured, a wicked glint in his eyes. 'But the good news is,' he said, sliding his palms under her dress and making her thighs quiver. 'Even if we hit the jackpot tonight, I still have a few months to practice.'

'I've got a better idea,' she said, sending him a saucy grin as she leaned close, tasting her own chocolate cupcakes and desire on his breath. 'Why don't I save you the trouble?' Running her palms over broad shoulders, she gazed deep into his emerald eyes. 'Callum

Westmore, will you marry me and give me your babies?'

Lifting her in his arms, his hands caressing her bottom as she wrapped her legs round his waist, he swung her round in a circle, kissed her full on the lips, and then laughed.

'Damn it, woman. I thought you'd never ask.'

As it turned out, it took them three months to hit the jackpot, by which time Cal had already got Ruby's signature on their marriage certificate. So the following Spring, when the proud parents celebrated the birth of Max Ryan Westmore with a cupcake and champagne picnic on Hampstead Heath, everyone was happy. Except Ruby, who—despite the addition of another six pounds that she would also have to lose at a later date—was ecstatic.

The Privileged and the Damned
by Kimberly Lang

Lily needs a fresh start—and, fingers crossed, she's found one. After all, why would any of the hot-shot Marshall dynasty even *think* to look beyond her humble façade? Until she catches the roving eye of infamous heartbreaker Ethan Marshall...

The Big Bad Boss
by Susan Stephens

Heath Stamp, the ultimate bad-boy-done-good, is now rich, arrogant and ready to raze his family estate to the ground. If Bronte tries to stop him he'll happily take her down with him. For Heath Stamp has gone from bad...to irresistible!

Ordinary Girl in a Tiara
by Jessica Hart

Caro Cartwright's had enough of romance—she's after a quiet life. Until an old school friend begs her to stage a gossip-worthy royal diversion! Reluctantly, Caro prepares to masquerade as a European prince's latest squeeze...

Tempted by Trouble
by Liz Fielding

Upon meeting smooth-talking Sean McElroy, Elle's 'playboy' radar flashes red, and she tries to ignore the traitorous flicker of attraction! Yet are these two misfits the perfect match?

On sale from 3rd June 2011
Don't miss out!

Available at WHSmith, Tesco, ASDA, Eason and all good bookshops

www.millsandboon.co.uk

MILLS & BOON®

are proud to present our...

Book of the Month

Come to Me
by Linda Winstead Jones

from Mills & Boon® Intrigue

Lizzie needs PI Sam's help in looking for her lost
half-sister. Sam's always had a crush on Lizzie.
But moving in on his former partner's daughter
would be *oh-so-wrong*…

Available 15th April

Something to say about our Book of the Month?
Tell us what you think!

millsandboon.co.uk/community
facebook.com/romancehq
twitter.com/millsandboonuk

GIVE IN TO TEMPTATION…

As the champagne flows beneath the glittering sun,
three scandalous affairs ignite…

It's going be one wickedly hot summer of sin!

Available 3rd June 2011

www.millsandboon.co.uk

11/25/MB339

2 FREE BOOKS
AND A SURPRISE GIFT

We would like to take this opportunity to thank you for reading this Mills & Boon® book by offering you the chance to take TWO more specially selected books from the Riva™ series absolutely FREE! We're also making this offer to introduce you to the benefits of the Mills & Boon® Book Club™—

- **FREE home delivery**
- **FREE gifts and competitions**
- **FREE monthly Newsletter**
- **Exclusive Mills & Boon Book Club offers**
- **Books available before they're in the shops**

Accepting these FREE books and gift places you under no obligation to buy, you may cancel at any time, even after receiving your free books. Simply complete your details below and return the entire page to the address below. You don't even need a stamp!

YES Please send me 2 free Riva books and a surprise gift. I understand that unless you hear from me, I will receive 4 superb new books every month for just £3.99 each, postage and packing free. I am under no obligation to purchase any books and may cancel my subscription at any time. The free books and gift will be mine to keep in any case.

Ms/Mrs/Miss/Mr _____ Initials _____

Surname _____

Address _____

_____ Postcode _____

E-mail _____

Send this whole page to: Mills & Boon Book Club, Free Book Offer, FREEPOST NAT 10298, Richmond, TW9 1BR

Offer valid in UK only and is not available to current Mills & Boon Book Club subscribers to this series. Overseas and Eire please write for details. We reserve the right to refuse an application and applicants must be aged 18 years or over. Only one application per household. Terms and prices subject to change without notice. Offer expires 31st July 2011. As a result of this application, you may receive offers from Harlequin (UK) and other carefully selected companies. If you would prefer not to share in this opportunity please write to The Data Manager, PO Box 676, Richmond, TW9 1WU.

Mills & Boon® is a registered trademark owned by Harlequin (UK) Limited.
Riva™ is being used as a trademark. The Mills & Boon® Book Club™ is being used as a trademark.